DIAMOND *of the*
SEASON

Diamond of the Season, Heiress, Book 1
Copyright © 2025 by Tamara Gill
Cover Art by Wicked Smart Designs
Editor Grace Bradley Editing, LLC
Published by: Tamara Gill Author
PO BOX 136, Gladstone, SA, Australia 5473
tamaragillauthor@gmail.com
ISBN: 978-1-923245-75-4 (trade paperback)

CHAPTER
ONE

1801, Hampshire

Rosalind muffled a curse and fisted her hands at her sides. Anger thrummed through her, and yet there would be no reprieve, no solace to be found for what she had just heard. It was so typical of her father to have done this last, awful thing to them—one final attempt to make their lives more miserable than they already were.

She kicked a stone, wincing as the thin, worn leather of her shoe provided no barrier to the sharp pebble. She cursed again, her fingernails bit into her palms. Would this day get any worse? She didn't think so, but the sight of a carriage coming along the gravel drive told her otherwise.

Who would call on them on the day of the reading of their father's will? A reading she could not stomach and was thankful when it was over.

Needing to escape outdoors and away from her devastated sisters' faces, she decided on a walk to clear her thoughts. To sit by and see all their hopes, their hearts crushed yet again by a parent who despised them all for not being the boys he wanted, the boys he needed to carry on his dukedom that he loved far more than anyone else, even their poor departed mama was beyond reprehensible of their parent.

She stopped and shaded her eyes as she took in the vehicle, having forgotten to grab her bonnet to save her complexion from the sun. Her mouth pursed into a displeased line. No doubt, it was the new Duke of Ravensmere, Earl Harrow as he was also known, come to claim his inheritance —her home—that was now his for the taking.

He would probably kick them all out on their ears, demanding they leave his new estate, even if he were to be their new guardian. Whoever thought that they, fully grown women all of them but their youngest sibling, Lady Clementine—but then she was only a year away from eighteen, so not so small any longer—would be under the authority of a stranger.

Rosalind kept walking, or stalking more like, unwilling to greet Lord Harrow before she was well and truly in the right mind to do so. He could go hang, as far as she was concerned right at this moment, along with her father's lawyer, who like their departed papa, saw them as more of six pests than human beings.

Bastards.

The reading of the will earlier that day had explained everything. None of the six daughters —her and her sisters—would inherit anything. Instead, everything would go to Lord Nathaniel Harrow, an earl from London with his own country estate in Surrey. He wasn't even a relative. In fact, he was such a distant connection he might as well have been born on the moon.

How was she to be civil to such a man? Arriving on the very day they had laid their father to rest in the family mausoleum and had the will read. The man was acting like a vulture swooping over a carcass that was barely cold.

She sighed and kicked another stone, sending it careening down the hillside. Her sisters had taken the news with calm dignity, much better than she. But as the eldest, Rosalind understood more of the implications. Their father had left them nothing—no dowry, not even their mother's jewelery. How she would have loved a trinket from the only person who loved them for who they were. Her dearest mama. How she wished she were here on a day like today.

Their only option, as the solicitor had explained, was to live in Scotland with their great-aunt Camilla. But the thought of leaving her beloved county of Hampshire for the cold, remote climes of Scotland was too much to bear.

She couldn't think that far ahead—not yet. First, they were to meet Lord Nathaniel Harrow and see what they could make of him. Perhaps he would show some kindness to his wards now that they were to be under his care. Mayhap the man was elderly and would relish the thought of having daughters he could care for.

Perhaps she was being too fanciful and needed to rein in her hopes and think realistically for her and her sisters. There was little point hoping for a better future when one did not yet know the character of the person who held all their lives in his hands.

She wandered the hills for some time—probably longer than she should have. It was rude of her to avoid the new Duke of Ravensmere, as he was now known, but her skin prickled at the thought of being civil to the gentleman just yet. Instead, Rosalind climbed over stiles and visited two tenant farmers on the outskirts of the estate, thanking them for their kind wishes and heartfelt condolences.

Not that she imagined many truly mourned her father. He had been a gruff, cruel man. Several estate buildings had needed repairs for years, and the tenants had long requested new roofs, only to be ignored. But her father, too busy enjoying the diversions of London, had dismissed the "petty dealings" of the poor.

As the sun dipped low, casting golden shadows across the fields, Rosalind headed home.

Candlelight glowed from the house windows as the staff moved through their evening tasks, drawing curtains and closing shutters. The sight of it sent a pang through her chest. All of this belonged to a stranger now. How unfair life was not to grant women the same privileges of men. Merely because she was born a girl, she must leave, move over for a man who did not love her beautiful home, or pretty lands. Or know the workers who toiled over the fields until their knuckles were bare to keep the home farms profitable.

She entered the foyer, handing her coat and gloves to a waiting footman.

"His Grace is waiting for you, Lady Rosalind," the footman said. "He's in the library, my lady."

"Thank you, James." Rosalind started toward the library. The door stood slightly ajar, and the flickering fire cast shifting shadows on the walls. She knocked once and a deep voice, much lower than her father's, bid her enter.

It felt strange to hear another man's voice coming from the room, after all these years of only ever knowing her father to occupy the space. When he bothered to travel home and make use of it.

She stepped inside. The high wing-backed chair was turned away, obscuring him from view. Steeling herself, she waited by the desk, knowing she would need to curtsy in propriety's name, though she resented the act.

He turned.

And for a moment, Rosalind forgot to breathe.

This was Lord Nathaniel Harrow—the vulture come to take everything they owned, simply because her parents had not produced a son. This was the new Duke of Ravensmere. Somehow she pictured the gentleman to be like her father in looks and stature.

How very wrong she was...

His Grace's dark gaze met hers, narrowing slightly in thought. "I presume you are the eldest, Lady Rosalind," he said.

She watched as he shuffled some papers, slipping a quill into an inkpot before signing a ledger. What possible business could he have already? He had only just inherited. Had he brought his own bookkeeping with him?

"I am, Your Grace." Rosalind dipped into a stiff curtsy, forcing her features to be welcoming and not displeased. How galling it was to have a stranger question who she was in her own home. The house she was born in and should have inherited. "Welcome to Ebonmere Abbey." How she managed to spit out those words and have them come out as sweetly as they sounded she would never know. Mayhap she should be on the stage instead of rusticating in the country.

He leaned back in his chair, studying her. Was he pleased with what he saw or merely tolerating her presence? She could not tell.

"Thank you for the warm welcome." His voice dripped with irony.

Perhaps he did sense a little of her displeasure. Not suitable for the stage after all. "I hope you've met my sisters."

"Yes. They were very polite and welcomed me kindly. I am sorry for the loss of your father."

She gestured to a chair. "May I sit, Your Grace?"

"Of course."

She perched on the edge of the seat, hands settled carefully in her lap as she chose her next words carefully. "While I thank you for your condolences, my father was a cruel man, most especially to his daughters," she said bluntly, seeing no reason to hide her disgust regarding her parent a moment longer. He had been awful to them, never a kind word, or gesture of love. Just resentment and disappointment. "And while I understand the rules when it comes to someone's passing, please do not think we're in a state of mourning. We may be wearing black, but that is for propriety's sake only." She paused. "But what I would like to discuss is what do you intend to do now that you have inherited the estate? And us—his daughters—along with it?"

He rubbed a hand over his jaw, drawing her attention to the strong, angular cut, covered in a day's growth of stubble. Had he been traveling long? London was only three days away by carriage. Surely, he could have stopped at an inn to refresh himself.

"Before you stormed out of the reading of the will—"

She raised her brows. Which sister or servant had informed him of that? "Again, Your Grace, I disagreed often with my father. But if I missed something important, I trust you will enlighten me."

"As a matter of fact, you did miss something."

Her curiosity piqued before he continued.

"There was one large caveat that you did not hear. I have inherited the dukedom, which grants me the title of Ravensmere and the entailed estates. However, your father did not leave you as destitute as you believe. He left each of you a considerable dowry."

Her breath caught. "A dowry?" That could not be true. Her father would never have been capable of such budgeting, or for that matter, love for his daughters. He'd always ensured they wore gowns that were three seasons out of date, and never new. They were the poorest-looking ducal daughters in England, Rosalind was sure.

"Yes, a dowry. Ten thousand pounds apiece. The funds are not directly under your control, but held in trust by me. Had you stayed long enough to hear the entire reading of the will, you would have heard you're now an heiress and quite capable of creating a future that is not dictated by me or your father, but yourself. If it pleases you to do so."

Her mouth opened, then closed. Did it please her to do so? To make choices and win the heart of a gentleman who loved her, and would make all her dreams come true.

Well, of course it pleased her.

"In any case," he continued, "with that dowry, each of your sisters will have a Season in the coming years. You, Lady Rosalind, will go first, since you are the eldest. Additionally, as I am instructed to be your and your sisters' guardian, I will ensure that all arrangements are made for your entrance into London society to be a success."

A dowry! Papa never mentioned such a thing... "Are you certain, Your Grace?"

"It is written on the parchment in the library desk drawer if you must read it." His tone was matter-of-fact, as though her astonishment were of little consequence and sense. The man clearly had never met her papa.

Rosalind scoffed, unable to hide the bite of sarcasm in her response.

"I know you weren't interested in the reading of the will earlier, but it is there in black and white. The ink has dried. Perhaps your father was not as terrible as you thought, my lady."

Delusional. The man was clearly delusional. Her father had never cared for any of them. They were not the sons he had craved.

"And we are to go to London for a Season?" she asked, still trying to grasp the shift in their circumstances.

"You are," he confirmed, standing and walking over to the fire. He pulled the bell pull with a sharp tug. "We have one month here at the estate, and then we shall leave for London. I shall hire a companion as a chaperone. And if fortune favors, you should be married by the end of it all."

Marriage. The thought of it was not without appeal. A home of her own, a future where she could ensure her sisters made their debuts. But such security hung on finding a suitable match— preferably a wealthy one. A man who was kind, who was nothing like her father.

The new Duke Ravensmere—though polite— seemed unbending, distant, and somewhat cold. He did not welcome the arrangement of guardian any more than she did.

"Do my sisters know?" she asked.

"Yes. They were pleased. Surprised, as you are."

She arched a brow. "It is astonishing, indeed. I had not thought father had left us anything."

"Was there anything else, Lady Rosalind, that you wish to discuss? If not, you may leave." His tone made it clear—this conversation had reached its end.

"Just one more thing—do you intend to stay with us for the next month?"

"I am your guardian. I did not expect to have six wards thrust upon me, but it is done. And I shall manage you all to the best of my ability."

Rosalind rose, dipping into a curtsy. "Thank you, Your Grace, for the clarification. I will bid you good afternoon if you will excuse me."

"You are excused," he said without looking up from the fire he now stood before.

Rosalind left swiftly, her steps light as she hurried up the stairs to her sisters' apartments. Their eyes widened as she entered, their excitement mirroring hers.

"Sister, did you hear? We have a dowry!" Evangeline exclaimed.

"Papa wasn't as heartless as we thought," Isabella murmured. "Perhaps he mellowed before his passing, even if we never saw it."

Rosalind shut the door, joining them all before the fire. "Perhaps. And it is good news. I shall find a match in London, and then I shall send for all of you. We will be together, and I will see each of you married and happy."

"What do you think of the new duke?" her youngest sister Clementine asked, her grin mischievous. "Is he not deadly handsome?"

"Oh yes, his eyes!" Cordelia said, sighing and flopping back onto the Aubusson rug for dramatics. "So green and beautiful."

"His shoulders and height! I swear my mouth dried at the sight of him when he strolled into the room during the reading of the will," Angelica said, a light blush on her cheeks.

"Handsome, indeed," Rosalind admitted. "But he does not seem overly pleased to have six young women under his care. He will tolerate us, but I would not say he's pleased that we come with the title."

"That is true," Evangeline said. "Perhaps he will warm to us—so long as we do not vex him too much."

"Unlikely," Angelica sighed. "We are forever in some sort of trouble."

Rosalind chuckled. "I look forward to London —the gowns, the dancing, the courtships."

"You must ride in Hyde Park!" Clementine said. "Perhaps a gentleman will take you out on one of their fine steeds. Maybe you will gallop on Rotten Row."

Rosalind laughed. "Perhaps now, galloping isn't allowed, remember. But with ten thousand pounds each, we may be able to choose our suitors rather than settle for less than we deserve. Or worse, must live in Scotland with Aunt Camilla." She shuddered at the thought. "I shall be one of the oldest debutantes, but at least I have a dowry to soften that disadvantage."

"True," Angelica agreed. "And you are one of the prettiest women in England."

"Don't be absurd," Rosalind corrected her. She had never thought herself particularly pretty. She was tall, her features strong rather than delicate, and she had a will that did not always endear her to men. A fishwife in the making, some might say. And at three-and-twenty, she was hardly an ideal debutante age.

"His Grace..." she mused. "If we keep our distance, I suspect we shall all get along just fine until I leave for London."

"London! I wish I could go now," Angelica said. "But in two years, I shall join you. How wonderful it will be!"

"Indeed. We should all practice our dancing, our etiquette."

"Especially you, Clementine," Cordelia teased. "You do love to slurp your soup."

"I do not do it on purpose!" Clementine protested. "I simply love soup."

Rosalind laughed. "How dear you all are. And to think—we feared we would be sent to Scotland. How dreary that would have been."

"Indeed. But it is getting late. We should prepare for dinner."

"Yes," Rosalind agreed. "We must be on our best behavior. His Grace is stuck with us, and we ought to prove to him that we are not a burden. We must make him like us, if we can."

"Yes!" Isabella said, ushering the younger sisters toward the door. "Put on your best dresses, girls. We must make an effort this evening."

"We do not have the finest," Rosalind murmured. "But we shall make do." She smiled at them all, hopeful for their future at last.

CHAPTER
TWO

Nathaniel sat at the table, his displeasure impossible to hide as he surveyed the so-called fruit platter, which was meant to double as a decoration.

It looked far from appealing.

The fruit appeared a week old—browned apples, overripe pears, and grapes that were starting to rot. One in particular looked like it had given up the fight and was laying half-inflated. This would never do. There was much to change in this estate now that it was his and he couldn't fathom the late duke being so indifferent to what was happening back at his home. Did the man truly not care for anything or anyone?

Seated at the head of the table, he waited for his six wards. Women whom he had not expected to come with the estate to join him. Not that they could help being left behind, forgotten by their turk of a father. But no matter what the duke had envisioned for his children, Nathaniel could not allow that to pass. He was Ravensmere now, and they were his responsibilities, and with that decision and honor, he'd ensured they would each receive a dowry. He could let them believe that their father had, during his final months, finally thought of them, and he would not disabuse them of their small pleasure.

After several minutes, and a glass of wine later, each of the six ladies strolled in one by one, entirely unconcerned that he had been waiting the past quarter-hour. Each of them sat, settling their skirts and smiling pleasantly in his direction.

His guard went up.

"Good evening," they murmured as they settled their napkins on their laps.

He nodded. "Good evening," he returned, wondering why he had the sense that they were up to something.

The eldest, Lady Rosalind Ravensmere, sat in the chair to his left. She reached for her glass of water and took a small sip and offered him a pleasant smile.

He wasn't sure what to make of her. Of all his wards, she was particularly sharp, he believed, and would not take fools lightly. She was also beautiful, certainly. But there was something about her that put him on guard. Independent.

Opinionated, without a qualm. He had no doubt she would make her opinion clear if she thought it appropriate.

But she was also fiercely protective of her sisters. He could tell by the way she watched them as they settled in for their meal, offering small smiles of encouragement, ensuring they were comfortable.

Once everyone was seated, he gestured for the footman to commence serving. The first course arrived, and once again, it failed to meet his standards.

He studied the dish of oxtail soup, unsure if it was even what it was supposed to be. Had it been cooked properly? Was it meant to look like dishwater? He pushed his plate away. A footman, ever observant, removed it immediately.

A good thing, too.

The sisters ate, their conversation quiet and subdued—nothing that caught his interest. But then, women's talk rarely intrigued him.

Once the estate was properly run, and a governess had been hired to guide the younger ladies here who would remain at the estate, along with a companion for Lady Rosalind for the Season, he would leave and wait for her arrival in London.

"We hope you've settled in, Your Grace," Lady Rosalind said, spooning up her meal without hesitation, as though there were nothing wrong with what had been served.

He watched her lift a spoonful of food to her lips and fought to school his expression. As much as he could revel in the sight of her pretty mouth, the meal itself was far from appealing.

"I am settling in well, thank you."

"I hope the estate ledgers are not in too terrible condition," she said. "Our father's steward did his best to manage everything without father's guidance."

"They are in better standing than I thought they would be, and I do not think it will be long before I have everything running just as I do at my other estate." There was no need to tell Lady Rosalind that there was very little money left, and the reason the estate had far fewer servants than it required was proof of that. Had the ladies of the house not noticed the dusty furniture, the lacklustre meals, and cold rooms? Perhaps they were so used to the conditions they had been living in that they merely did not notice.

She threw him a small smile. "Father rarely came here in the last years of his life. In fact, I do believe it had been five years since he'd celebrated Yuletide here before he passed."

"Indeed, he did not," Lady Evangeline confirmed. "It has indeed been five years since he spent Christmas here. I have it written in my journal."

Nathaniel considered their words. The late

Duke of Ravensmere had been an odd man, cold and distant, even to London. In fact, he could count on one hand how many gentlemen the duke spoke to at Whites. It was a wonder his daughters had turned out as warm and kind to one another as they were. But perhaps that was the reason—they had found love, companionship, and guidance in one another, rather than in their father.

"Do you think you will spend Christmas here, Your Grace?" one of the younger sisters, Clementine he believed, asked.

"Possibly," he said. "I have another estate in Surrey that demands my time, but now that Ravensmere is mine, I suppose I must divide my attention between the two."

"Do you think we might return for Christmas and holidays?" Isabella asked. "This is our home. We would be loath to lose it completely once we are married."

Nathaniel nodded. He saw no issue with the ladies visiting their childhood home—so long as he was not there. They could enjoy their reunions without his presence well enough.

"That would be perfectly acceptable. I can arrange for the staff to be prepared whenever you wish to return. Though be aware, I may not always be present."

He met Rosalind's gaze and realized she was studying him. Was that disappointment in her eyes? Surely not, what would she care if he returned here when they were present or not.

The first course was cleared away, replaced with a much more palatable second course.

"May I ask," Rosalind ventured, "what your London home is like, Your Grace? We have never been to London—not a one of us. Papa never took us, you see. But we are eager to know what the Season will be like."

Nathaniel suppressed a sigh. He had no desire to discuss London or all its diversions. But he supposed he had little choice. The women, for all their manners and perfect deportment he'd noticed so far, were far from ready for their debut. They would be the greenest and oldest debutantes in town.

"It is busy," he said simply, turning his attention to his meal. "Many people and carriages, you must all take care when having an outing."

He felt Rosalind's gaze on him, but he offered no further elaboration. London was vastly different from the countryside. He spent most of his time in clubs, rarely attending balls. As for Almack's? Well, he would rather expire of boredom than attend that cesspit. But now, he supposed, he would have to go and do right by his ward.

"Do you have a busy social life in London, Your Grace?" the youngest sister, Clementine asked. "Will we be hosting balls or simply attending them?"

"Oh yes, do tell us, Your Grace," Angelica added. "I am twenty this year. If Rosalind finds a match, it will not be long before I make my debut."

"Are we not all going to be the oldest debutantes in London?" Evangeline said dryly. "How humiliating that shall be, but a necessary evil I suppose."

Nathaniel ate more quickly, eager for the meal to end. He did not wish to be interrogated or bombarded with questions over the Season further.

"Are you pleased with inheriting, Your Grace?" Rosalind asked at last. "As much as Mama tried, she never had a son—only us six girls. So..." She paused. "Becoming a Duke must be exciting, I imagine."

Nathaniel cleared his throat, not wanting to repeat what he'd said the moment he was informed. Such curses were not for ladies' ears, but it had been only from mere shock. That and the following shock at finding out how very poor the title was. "I was surprised, Lady Rosalind, to be the first in line for the title."

"Well, we think you shall do a very fine job, Your Grace. We cannot thank you enough for taking us on and supporting us through our Seasons in town. That father thought of us in his final days is a great comfort, and he would be pleased to know his heir is an upstanding and thoughtful man."

Nathaniel drained his wine and pushed back his chair. He was not an upstanding man. Hell, in London he had a reputation for being quite the opposite, especially when it came to the opposite sex. He was a bachelor, and now with two titles, his popularity would be twofold. Having to escort Lady Rosalind about town would also place him in social situations he had avoided up until now. For all his delight at being a duke, it also had it downfalls.

"Excuse me, my ladies. Enjoy your evening." He left swiftly, keeping his gaze forward and not at the shocked, and dare he say it, hurt expressions of his wards. His hurried steps did not halt until he was ensconced in the sanctuary of the library. He shut the door and locked it, hoping to end any further conversations for the night. Who knew women could talk so much or ask so many questions. He was utterly exhausted.

And he would have to do it all again tomorrow.

The thought was like a death knell in his mind.

CHAPTER
THREE

Later that evening, Nathaniel, seated at his desk, heard the soft, melodic strains of the pianoforte drifting from the ballroom. He placed his quill aside, leaned back in his chair, and allowed the music to wash over him. It was Beethoven, though he could not place the specific piece. Regardless, it transported him, offering a momentary respite from his responsibilities.

Curiosity got the better of him. Rising from his chair, he strode toward the ballroom, drawn by the skillful playing. As he approached, he saw the door slightly ajar and paused, standing in the shadows as he observed Lady Rosalind at the piano. She was utterly lost to the world, her fingers gliding over the keys with ease, her expression serene.

He debated turning away, but as her guardian, it was prudent to know her talents—

such accomplishments were invaluable in securing a good match. At least, that was what he told himself. Steeling his mettle, he pushed the door open and strolled into the ballroom, only halting when he was beside the piano.

"You play very well, Lady Rosalind." He leaned against the instrument until she finished her song. "Pray tell, do your sisters share your talent?"

Rosalind ran her fingers lightly over the ivory keys, seemingly marveling at the fine craftsmanship of the pianoforte before gently closing the lid. She lifted her gaze to meet his, and for the first time since they had been introduced, he noticed how striking her dark-blue eyes were—almond-shaped and framed by long lashes. Confidence and intelligence shone within them, and for a fleeting moment, he found himself taken aback. With the distractions of dinner, even sitting beside her, he'd not taken in her appearance much, but now...

"My youngest sister, Lady Clementine, also enjoys playing, but my other sisters do not share our enthusiasm," she replied. "They prefer embroidery and painting, though none of us are masters of any art." She smiled wistfully before adding, "We have always been more inclined toward the outdoors—riding, exploring, and caring for our animals, much to our father's dismay. It is likely the reason we are all plagued with freckles."

Nathaniel's gaze dipped to her nose, noting the faint dusting of freckles across her fair skin. She was undeniably beautiful, and that thought alone unsettled him. He straightened, pushing the notion aside.

"Your piano playing will certainly serve you well in London," he said. "And what of dancing? Are you all proficient, or shall I engage a dance master to instruct you?"

"Oh no, we can all dance, my lord...I mean, Your Grace," she assured him, though she had momentarily forgotten his newly inherited title. "We were raised with all the proper etiquette expected for a London Season by our dearest mama before she passed. You need not concern yourself."

"Very good." He hoped he did not. Without thinking, Nathaniel extended his hand. "Perhaps we should test your dancing abilities. Shall we?"

Her eyes widened, but after a brief hesitation, she stood, adjusting her gown and smoothing the fabric before stepping closer.

What the hell am I doing? She's your ward, man. No need to dance with the chit.

He debated withdrawing the invitation, but it was too late. He had come to assess her abilities, not to dance with her. And yet, as she stepped into his arms, the warmth of her body and the gentle swish of her gown against his legs made him acutely aware of how long it had been since he had last held a woman whom he had not paid for her services. A woman of quality and breeding.

Before coming to the country, he had been too consumed by the demands of his estate to warrant entering society and trying to find an acceptable wife. Now, in a house filled with six young women, the eldest one distracting him most, that absence was becoming far too apparent.

He led them into a waltz, testing her skill, and as she moved with ease, he could not help but admire her grace. She was an exceptional dancer, far surpassing his expectations. When she looked up at him, a small smile playing on her lips, he found himself struck by her beauty.

This was wrong.

He was her guardian, tasked with ensuring she found a suitable match. It did not matter that there were only a few years between them. He had been entrusted with her care, not to entertain improper thoughts.

"You will have many admirers in London, Lady Rosalind." He broke the silence at last. "With your dowry and beauty, you shall have no shortage of suitors. Tell me, what sort of gentleman do you hope to wed?"

She considered his question carefully before

replying, "A kind man. One who values me for more than my dowry, who is not cruel or overbearing. I could not bear to be married to a man with a mistress."

Nathaniel inclined his head. "A worthy desire, though not always an easy one to fulfill. Many gentlemen maintain mistresses while keeping their wives in respectable spheres."

She frowned, a light blush kissing her cheeks. "Then I would live in regret of my choice."

Something about her quiet certainty unsettled him. She deserved better than that, of course. He had seen the fate of too many wives cast aside by their unfaithful husbands. The idea of Rosalind suffering such a fate did not sit well with him. Even though he enjoyed having a whore in his bed, he had always favored the idea of marrying a woman who would fulfil his needs, and such extramarital affairs were not required.

"I will do my utmost to guide you toward a good match, one who will not bring you such regrets."

She smiled up at him and his breath hitched. When she smiled, her whole face transformed, her eyes lighting up with trust and sparkling prettily under the candlelight.

"That is very kind of you, Your Grace. I do hope the gentlemen do not find me too old."

"Too old?" he scoffed. "You are three-and-twenty, the perfect age to make a thoughtful decision. At eighteen, one is far too young to understand the weight of marriage. I was reckless and arrogant at that age. No one should have wished me for a husband."

"I suppose you are right. And I thank you for your honesty."

She hesitated, then added, "A dear friend of mine married young, but her husband now spends most of his time in London, while she remains in the country with their children. I do not wish for such a fate."

Nathaniel nodded. "We shall ensure you make a wise choice, Lady Rosalind."

They continued their waltz, and he found himself momentarily forgetting the impropriety of their dance even without the music to guide them. She fit well in his arms, her movements instinctive and elegant. She would do exceedingly well in London.

"And what of you, Your Grace?" she asked. "Are you seeking a wife?"

"I am not actively looking, but if I meet a lady who meets my requirements, I shall consider it."

She smiled wryly. "Then may we both find happiness and contentment."

"Indeed."

He spun her to a graceful stop and bowed. "I shall see you in the morning for our ride to the tenant farms."

"Yes, Your Grace. Thank you." She gave him a

small smile, and for several long seconds, he found himself unable to look away.

Shaking himself from his reverie, he strode from the ballroom and returned to his library, ensuring he shut the door firmly behind him.

He slumped against it, frowning. What the bloody hell was he doing?

He had gone to observe her musical talent, not to dance with her. And yet, he had done so willingly. Worse, he had enjoyed it.

That could not happen again.

He was her guardian. His duty was to see her wed, not to entertain inappropriate thoughts. He would ensure Lady Rosalind's and her siblings' Seasons were a success, and he would not stand in their way—or, worse, place himself in their path.

FOUR

The following morning, Rosalind rode out with the new duke, determined to show him the estate she loved so very dearly and ensure repairs for the tenant farmers got underway. He seemed an affable man, the sort of gentleman who would take care of the land and the people working it. Not a small task, considering the estate was vast, with extensive grounds, hundreds of acres of forest, perfect for deer and game to thrive. A hunting lodge that her grandfather had built and used often—though her father had barely used it.

By the time they reached the stables, the horses were ready.

"I've settled Breeze for you, Your Grace," the stable hand said. "Thought you may want to try one of the estate horses today. He should do well enough for you around the grounds."

"Very well, thank you," the duke said, before

mounting his horse with effortless grace, his strong thighs flexing as he settled in the saddle. The horse was at least seventeen hands high, but it seemed to make no difference to him.

Rosalind watched him, impressed despite herself. Then, with a nod to the stable hand, she used his assistance to mount—though today she had no intention of riding side saddle.

The duke raised a brow at her choice but said nothing. Instead, he turned his horse toward the stable yard gates.

"This way, Your Grace. We'll head west first and check in on Mr. Arthur before he gets too busy for the day."

"Of course. I'll follow your lead."

They set off, Rosalind considering what to say. The duke wasn't one for idle chatter, but he was kind. The fact he'd agreed to come out and see the issues her father had left behind said a lot about his character.

"We have deer and pheasant on the grounds, Your Grace. You're welcome to invite guests to stay and hunt. The rooms are always ready. My father never made much use of the estate, but the staff keeps everything prepared, just in case."

"Good to know," he said. "Do you hunt, Lady Rosalind?"

She turned to look at him as they rode along a well-worn path through the forest, dappled sunlight filtering through the branches. The air still held a lingering chill from winter, but the scent of spring was beginning to stir.

"I do, Your Grace. I've ridden since I was a child. Before my mother died, she insisted that all her daughters learn. Though three of my sisters loathe the sport, I've always believed that as long as the animal doesn't suffer and nothing goes to waste, then hunting is acceptable. People must eat, after all."

"A practical view."

She nodded, unsure if he approved or merely found her stance interesting or was completely bored by the conversation they were having. It was hard to tell with the man.

"I met your father once in London," he added. "I wouldn't claim to have known him well, but one might have assumed he had no home at all for the time he spent at his clubs."

Rosalind mulled over his words. It confirmed what she'd long suspected—her father had barely spent any time at home. And if the rumors were true, he had kept a mistress in his final years. Had her father's mistress been left with anything when he passed? She doubted it. He wasn't the sort of man to part with money easily, not even for those closest to him. The fact that her own dowry had remained intact was an amazement.

"I'm surprised he never mentioned you would inherit, Your Grace. When you met him in

London," she said. "Surely he must have known our cousin had passed by then. He's been gone several years."

"If he did, he never said a word. Then again, he never had much to say to me—I was only an earl, after all."

Rosalind chuckled. "That does sound like my father. He was an elitist through and through."

They rode in companionable silence for a while until they reached a small clearing, where a thatched-roof cottage came into view. It was a pretty-enough house, two stories with glistening windows and a thin stream of smoke curling from the chimney.

"This is Mr. Arthur's cottage," Rosalind said. "He's one of the gamekeepers. Papa made him pay rent, even though he's an old man, and barely capable of a full day's work." She shook her head at the thought. Her father had made the old man continue to pay, despite his decades of loyalty and his failing health.

"Is he still currently paying it?" the duke asked.

"Yes, Your Grace. His income isn't what it once was, though, so...perhaps that could be amended." She didn't press the issue, but she could see the duke was already considering it. Had it been her choice, she would have stopped the requirement from Mr. Arthur. But the estate, while her home, did not belong to her, nor the running of it.

"I'll look over the ledgers and see what can be done. I haven't yet reviewed the estate's accounts, but you have my word—I'll take care of it."

"Thank you, Your Grace."

They pulled up in front of the cottage, and Mr. Arthur bustled outside, his weathered face breaking into a wide smile.

"Good morning, Lady Rosalind!" he called.

Rosalind dismounted and went to clasp his hands. "Mr. Arthur, I hope we find you well on this beautiful morning."

"Oh, well enough," he said. "Just put the kettle on—you're welcome to join me for a cup."

"Oh, that would be lovely, but first, may I introduce His Grace, the Duke of Ravensmere? He's inherited the estate from Father."

Mr. Arthur's eyes went wide, and he hurried to bow, though his old bones protested and he groaned. "Your Grace, an honor."

"How do you do, Mr. Arthur," the duke said politely.

"There's no need for that, Mr. Arthur," Rosalind said quickly, helping him back upright. "The duke is here to see the damage to the roof and thatch from the last storm. Perhaps we could look at the upstairs room?"

Mr. Arthur nodded eagerly. "Oh, that would

be a great help. Last night, I swear there was a rat in the house, scratching about in the empty room. I've had to move out of it, you know. And when it rains, the water just pours in! No matter how much I've tried to patch it, I cannot keep the vermin out."

"We'll take a look," the duke said. "If the roof's salvageable, we'll repair it. If not, we'll replace the structure entirely."

The old man blinked in surprise. "Oh, Your Grace...that's more than I dared hope."

"It is as it should be, Mr. Arthur."

Once inside, as promised, Mr. Arthur poured them tea. He sighed contentedly as he settled into his chair, his bones creaking loud enough that Rosalind heard them.

"I do cherish this house. My children were raised here. My dear wife... We were married in the local church, spent our whole lives here together before she passed last year."

"I can understand the sentiment," the duke said, his gaze drifting around the room before landing on Rosalind.

She held his gaze, trying to read his thoughts. Did he feel burdened by everything her father had left him? Or was he so wealthy that the cost of repairs meant nothing?

She would never know for sure. But the fact that he was here, listening, and willing to act— told her she'd been right to trust him.

After finishing their tea, they followed Mr. Arthur upstairs to assess the damage. The sight of the missing roof was worse than Rosalind remembered.

The duke shook his head. "How long has it been like this?" he asked, testing one of the rafters.

"Since last winter, Your Grace. The storm before the first snows took the roof clear off. I tried to gather the thatch and wood, but most were too scattered and broken to use."

"Very well. I'll send my steward with workers tomorrow. If the roof can't be salvaged, we'll replace it outright."

Mr. Arthur clutched Rosalind's hand, his eyes welling with tears. "Lady Rosalind? You are the best of them. Thank you for bringing the duke here today. I have hope, finally."

She squeezed his hand, swallowing the lump in her throat. "I'm sorry you had to live this way for so long."

Mr. Arthur sighed before leading them back downstairs. "As am I, my lady. But I do not hold you responsible, so enough of that."

They stepped outside, and Rosalind retrieved a wrapped bundle of food from her saddlebag. "Cook sent biscuits for you."

Mr. Arthur grinned, lifting the cloth parcel to his nose and breathing deep. "A new roof, my favorite biscuits, and I've met the Duke of Ravensmere—what a grand day!"

The duke chuckled, and for the first time, Rosalind saw him smile. A real, unguarded smile. And blast it all to Hades, he was a handsome gentleman when he did so.

Something fluttered low in her stomach. She swallowed hard and turned to her horse, trying to ignore the sensation.

"Come, Your Grace," she said, swinging into the saddle. "We've another tenant to visit."

And, if she wasn't careful, another problem to deal with—her sudden physical awareness of the Duke of Ravensmere.

CHAPTER
FIVE

They finished their day out and about at the tenant farms and lands of the Ravensmere estate only when the quaint village rooftops of Beaulieu came into view.

"Would you care to have luncheon in the tavern, Your Grace? They do a good stew, and the ale is said to be of good quality."

Nathaniel glanced at Lady Rosalind, unsure he'd heard her right. Tavern? Ale?

"Are you telling me that you drink ale, my lady?"

She laughed, and the sound washed over him like a soothing balm. She had a pretty laugh, and her face lit up like the morning light, warming everything in its path.

"I do not, but I thought that's what gentlemen drank when they darkened the doors of a tavern."

She smiled, waiting for him to decide if he would like to dine at the town tavern or not. The idea did have its allures, especially with the cook back at the estate. He hated to imagine what the cook had prepared and was dishing out to everyone.

He shuddered at the thought. "I think a luncheon in town would be just the thing, my lady. Lead the way."

Without further ado, Lady Rosalind turned her horse toward town and pushed her mount into a trot.

Nathaniel followed and realized his error the moment his ward lifted her pert ass up into the air and back down again with each step of the horse. For several heartbeats his eyes were fixated on her pert globes before she glanced behind—perhaps sensing his interest—and he forced his gaze over her shoulders and focused on the small steeple of the church.

It took minutes only, and they pulled their horses up to walk along the main thoroughfare of the village.

Several people milling about the streets stopped to look and wave. Several of them called out to Lady Rosalind, and she greeted them all by name with a pleasant return of address.

Was there no one that this daughter of the late duke did not know? He could not help but summarize that she had taken on the role of duke when her father wasn't around and did her best to keep her household staff, and those in the wider community happy and content.

A hard task when one did not have the financial means to help and only the moral ability to support.

They pulled up before the Duck and Dog tavern and tied their horses to the hitching posts provided. The inn, thankfully, was quiet as they entered the dining room, and a young barmaid—dressed in a nondescript brown muslin gown, her large rounded belly, no doubt from the later stages of pregnancy—waddled over to them with a welcoming smile on her face.

"Lady Rosalind, good day to you, my lady. It's a pleasure indeed to have you here. What can I get ya, love?" she asked, only throwing him a cursory glance.

Rosalind, like all the people that she encountered, smiled and reached out, clasping the young woman's hand quickly.

"A table for two, if you please. We're going to have luncheon here today." Lady Rosalind turned and gestured to him. "This is the new Duke of Ravensmere, Mary."

The young barmaid's eyes flew wide, and she dipped into an awkward curtsy.

"Your Grace, welcome to Beaulieu. What a pleasure and honor it is to serve you this afternoon."

Nathaniel waved her honors aside, not wanting to be singled out in front of the townspeople present. "I'm pleased to be here. Lady Rosalind speaks highly of your establishment. She says you do an awfully good stew."

"We do indeed." She gestured for them to follow. "Come, I shall seat you near the front window overlooking the town square. It's a prettier view than the inn's hitching yard."

They followed and were soon seated. It took minutes only before their food arrived—steaming, with a goodness that smelled as delicious as it looked. Nathaniel's stomach growled, and Lady Rosalind lifted her napkin to her lips and chuckled.

"I apologize. I seem to be more hungry than I thought."

"No need to apologize. I thought you might like to dine out today. I fear you're not coping as well as my sisters and I when it comes to Cook's cooking."

He cringed, picked up his spoon, and started to eat his stew. "You noticed, did you? I fear that you are indeed correct, and my gullet is suffering."

"I do apologize. Our cook has been with us since before my mother married my father. She's five-and-eighty this year, and I fear her cooking has become less than ideal. I fear you will have to replace her soon."

Nathaniel pondered Lady Rosalind's words and could hear the concern in her voice.

"If you think I shall kick her out without a living for the rest of her days, rest assured that is not the case. I will offer her a house on the estate; I'm sure there are some that are empty, even if in need of repair. She'll be well looked after."

He could feel her gaze on him, and, unable to resist looking at his striking ward, he glanced up from his stew. The unshed tears in her eyes made panic bolt through his blood, and instinctively he reached for her hand and clasped it. "What is wrong? Are you ill?"

"No, nothing of the kind." She held his hand in return and did not look to relinquish it any-time soon. "How lovely of you to be so caring. We're not used to such treatment, as you well know. I feared for our tenant farmers and the staff at the great house, but you are truly an angel sent from heaven. I'm so relieved you're not awful."

He laughed. "I'm relieved you do not find me so also."

Nathaniel took his hand back and resumed eating, ignoring the fact that his heart had kicked up several beats at Lady Rosalind's touch. The woman was uncommonly pretty and kind, and he feared he liked her far too much—more than he thought.

You're her guardian, remember. You promised to find her a good match.

A ruckus sounded in the bar just outside the room in which they were dining, before the door slammed open and several men stumbled and fell into the room. Shouts and several words no woman ought to hear rang out about the room.

Lady Rosalind gasped and stood, just in time, before a man in full fisticuffs with another flew through the air and landed on the bowl of stew— breaking the porcelain and the table, smashing their meal and table to pieces.

Before Nathaniel could get to her, a fist connected with his jaw. He stumbled back.

"What the bloody blazers is going on," he said, regaining his feet and trying to make sense of the brawl. When another went to attack him, possibly merely because he was nearby, he grabbed the fellow by the lapels of his coarse wool jacket and threw him a solid blow to his nose, watching with a little satisfaction as the man stumbled to the ground, out cold.

He could see Lady Rosalind attempting to make herself as small as possible in the corner, and all he could think was to get to her—to keep her safe.

She screamed as a man fell at her feet, attempting to pull himself up using her skirts.

The barman, a burly, large man carrying a

club, entered the room and started in on the arguing men.

Nathaniel grabbed the man who dared clutch at Lady Rosalind's skirts and ripped him off before going to her. She threw herself into his arms, holding him as if her life depended on his shelter.

And right at this moment, perhaps it did.

He pushed her into the corner, pressed her against the wall, and tried to keep them both as small and inconspicuous as possible.

She shivered in his arms, clearly terrified, and yet—damn his rakish soul—he could feel every curve of her body, the soft breasts pressing into his lower chest, her fingers clawing at his shirt beneath his jacket. The sensation was very much reminiscent of a sexual one, and he hated himself for enjoying having her this close to his person.

He was a cad and ought to be horsewhipped.

"Your Grace, your nose is bleeding."

She reached up and attempted to wipe the blood from his face, and the sensation of her hand cupping his jaw stilled his frantic heart.

Their eyes met and held, and no matter the noise behind him, he could not look away.

Her attention dipped to his lips, as his did to hers.

Damn it all to hell, *do not do it* was his last thought before he dipped his head.

CHAPTER

SIX

Rosalind stilled, her heart pounding frantically in her chest—a relentless pulse that would not abate—and she could not entirely place the blame on the fisticuffs unfolding around them.

Instead, the strong arms and warm, muscular body that held her close, cupped the back of her head, and pulled her into a warm, comforting embrace meant to keep her safe were the cause. She had never felt more on edge of a precipice than right at this moment, teetering before she fell. She had never been held by a man before, and never under such circumstances. Her body did not feel like itself; it tingled and grew warm, relaxed amongst the chaos, and became pliant in his arms.

If she closed her eyes, she could almost imagine His Grace holding her for a reason entirely different from a mere need to protect her—a tender embrace akin to that of a lover cradling the woman he adored.

Her hand slipped from his jaw, the stubble lightly scratching her palm—a sensation both new and not unpleasant. Thoughts swirled in her mind. What would his skin feel like against hers? Would his kiss be as soft and caring as his hold? Her gaze drifted to his lips, which were of a lovely shape; not overly plump for a man, but enough to emphasize his handsome mouth.

Her nerves somersaulted in her stomach, and she stilled when he dipped his head toward her. Was he going to kiss her here—in the tavern dining room, before a brawling group of ruffians?

Yes, please...

"Enough!" the innkeeper roared. Rosalind jumped as the room fell silent.

The interruption seemed enough to shake the duke's resolve. He reared back, turning around—but keeping her behind him—as he surveyed the room and the many men in various states of disarray.

"You are all banned from the tavern until I am no longer angry with you. Leave now, before I call the magistrate, and he puts all of you into the watch house."

The men, not wishing to get into trouble with the law, waddled out like scolded dogs with their tails between their legs, while others groaned as they regained their feet and followed suit.

"Your Grace, Lady Rosalind, how very sorry I am that your luncheon was ruined. I do profoundly apologize and hope that this incident does not stop you from dining here again."

Rosalind continued to cling to the back of the duke's coat, desperate to prolong the feel of him —his scent a blend of sandalwood and leather, no doubt acquired from their many hours of riding.

"Do not concern yourself," the duke said. "My nose will heal, and I'm certain that Lady Rosalind —while shocked and a little alarmed—is perfectly well. But we will take our leave. I hope there is not too much damage to your establishment, though I fear this room is grossly affected."

"You're very kind, Your Grace. Thank you. I shall see you both out."

Their horses were brought out from the stables—watered and groomed. She walked over to her mount, but before she could have the stable hand lead her horse to the mounting block, the duke came over and offered his assistance. He clasped his hands together, and she placed her foot into the makeshift stirrup. Holding on to the reins and saddle, she hoisted herself into her seat.

"Thank you, Your Grace."

He nodded without a word as he strode to his horse and climbed up without assistance. The man was athletic, and she doubted there was anything he could not do.

"Was there anywhere else you wished to escort me this afternoon, Lady Rosalind, or shall we return to the house?"

"I think home, Your Grace. Perhaps your valet would like to have a look at the mess your bloody nose has made of your attire." She glanced at his shirt, where droplets of blood stained the linen— a sight that suggested it would be best removed sooner rather than later.

"That is true. I do not need another telling-off for soiling my attire."

Had the new duke just attempted to make light of their altercation that afternoon? She smiled before pushing her mount out of the yard, and within the hour they had arrived back at the estate's stable. They spoke very little on the way home, except for the few times Rosalind pointed out the boundaries of the estate and the location of the hunting lodge nestled within the copse of trees they passed.

Once they returned their horses, they made their way back into the house.

"Thank you for today, Lady Rosalind. It is a credit to you that you are so invested in the people who work here and those who labor on the lands of the estate."

Warmth filled her at the duke's words. Not that she ever sought praise—she was never vain —but it was comforting to know that someone recognized her efforts, even if her father never had.

"It is the least I could do. I love this house, its lands, and the people who live here. I have grown up with everyone we spoke to today—they have been more present in my life than my own parents. How could I not care what happens to them? I am simply thankful that, now that I shall leave here, they will be well looked after. I would hate to marry and move to another county, knowing that the new duke was cut from a similar cloth as my father."

They strolled into the foyer and handed their hats, coats, and gloves to two waiting footmen.

"We saw you arriving from your ride, Your Grace, Lady Rosalind, and have set out some sandwiches and a hot cup of tea in the drawing room, should you care for a repast."

"Thank you, Dennis. That would be most welcome," she replied, especially since their luncheon had been smashed onto the floor by the brawling townsfolk.

"I shall meet you in there shortly, Lady Rosalind. I must change before we finish our luncheon."

"Of course."

Rosalind went into the drawing room and

took the opportunity to pour the tea and arrange several sandwiches on the small plates provided. The duke joined her after several minutes, now attired in a clean shirt and jacket. He sat beside her, and Rosalind had to admit she enjoyed having him so close.

"Thank you for serving. This looks good indeed."

"Yes," she replied, sipping her tea and watching him. "The cook's sandwiches never fail to please, even if she is somewhat wanting with other courses."

His eyes sparkled in amusement. "Wonderful."

They ate in silence, which gave Rosalind the opportunity to ponder how she had felt in the duke's arms in the tavern—and what that might mean. She liked him, she knew that. He was kind and not dismissive at all, so very different from the cold, lofty man she had imagined. He was warm and personable—a true breath of fresh air in their stagnant, grand lives.

"These are delicious indeed." The duke reached for several more sandwiches and placed them on his plate.

"They are, I agree, and I am sorry that our lovely lunch was so rudely brought to a halt. I was enjoying myself exceedingly."

"As was I." His gaze met hers, and Rosalind's skin prickled with awareness. He averted his eyes toward the windows, and she studied him, wondering if he, too, was feeling all sixes and sevens as she was—as if something were occurring between them, something she could not name. The duke might be more attuned to what was unfolding between them, but she was not—a predicament, she supposed, common among ladies who had not yet had their Season or been married.

After all, she had never been kissed, and she wondered whether her feelings for the duke were merely the budding of a platonic friendship or if the tumultuous emotions stirring inside her signaled the beginning of something that could blossom into so much more.

"I hope you were not injured, Lady Rosalind. I know several bodies crashed into us before I was able to reach you."

She shook her head and placed her teacup down on the small wooden table before them. "Not at all—merely startled, but not injured. Thank you for protecting me, Your Grace. You are very kind."

"I could not allow anything to happen to you, my lady. That would not be the act of a gentleman—or a friend, for that matter—which I believe we are becoming..."

"Indeed." Warmth spread through her at his words. "I believe we are too, and in the spirit of that friendship, please call me Rosalind. You are my guardian, after all, and I do not think we need to be so formal."

His mouth twisted into a wicked grin, and her stomach knotted. "Only if you call me Nathaniel in return."

CHAPTER
SEVEN

The following day, Rosalind woke to her maid Mary shaking her awake, a harried look on her face.

"Lady Rosalind. Wake up. There is news, and we must get you prepared."

Rosalind sat up and rubbed her face, focusing on her maid who was now darting about the room, pulling out her valise from her dressing room next door, before ruffling through the armoire as if the devil himself were after her.

"Whatever is this about? Has something happened?" Rosalind asked. Thankfully, despite Mary's worried countenance, she had not forgotten Rosalind's morning hot chocolate. Rosalind reached for the mug and took a lovely, fortifying sip to start the day. The chocolate drink was rich and creamy, sweet and delicious—just as she liked it.

"The duke has ordered me to pack your

things. You are to leave for London today with His Grace. I heard the butler mention that it has something to do with the duke needing to return to town early, so you are to travel with him. We must pack your things immediately, for fifteen minutes of the allotted hour have already passed." The maid paused her packing and raised her brow. "You are not the easiest lady to raise, as you well know."

Rosalind threw back her bedding and stepped from the bed, setting her hot chocolate aside. London! She was going to London. Never had she been to the great city, and the thought of starting her future—possibly finding a husband, a great love match that would outshine the greatest love stories in history—made excitement thrum through her.

"Well, I must dress. I will quickly finish my morning ablutions and then you may do my hair. It does not need to be anything grand, for I shall be in a carriage most of the day and no one will see me, in any case."

"Of course, my lady. I will continue to pack while you do so."

Before she could walk another step, Rosalind's door flew open and, one by one, her five sisters stumbled into the room, their faces a mix of sadness and excitement. Rosalind embraced each of them, wiping away the tears from

Clementine—the baby of the house whom she would miss and worry about most.

"I cannot believe you are to leave us, sister. We shall all miss you very much," Clementine said, pulling a handkerchief from her pocket and dabbing her eyes.

"Now, now, I shall not be gone forever, and should I make a match, I will discuss the possibility of you all coming to live with me so that we shall always be together."

"Do you think the duke would allow such a thing? He is our guardian now," Isabella said, slumping onto the bed with a dejected look on her pretty face.

"He's a kind man and does not want to see any of us unhappy, I do not believe. Even though he is only a few years older than I am, he is mature beyond his years and knows that we are far better together than apart."

"I do hope so, Lady Evangeline. And then, next year, when I am in town for the Season, you may be able to sponsor me, and I shall be with you. I should so hate not to be together."

"As would I, dearest, but I promise you all," Rosalind said, pulling her sisters into her arms and trying to gather them close. They hugged, clinging to one another as if they would never be separated.

But time waits for no one, and each of them,

when the time was right, would marry, move to their new homes, and create families for themselves. Rosalind swallowed the lump in her throat, knowing that from that day forward nothing would ever be the same for them—not really. She would be the first to leave, to try to forge some future happiness that had long been absent from their lives, but she would certainly not be the last.

She could hear several sniffles from her sisters and held them even tighter. "Do not worry so. I will write and tell you everything about town and all its diversions. It shall be as if I never left—I promise you all."

"Please do not forget us," Cordelia said, her eyes red-rimmed and tears pooling in her pretty green irises.

"Of course I will not. I promise on my life I shall write every week."

The thud of her trunk closing and her maid rushing over to the bellpull to ring for footmen caught her attention. Her time to get ready was ticking by. "Now, come, girls—let me finish getting ready for my travels, and we shall say our goodbyes downstairs very soon. But please, do not fret. As I said, if I should make a good match, I will send for you with the duke's permission. I am certain he does not wish for us to be apart any more than we do."

"I do hope you're right," Angelica said, giving a solemn glance before they all walked out the door and downstairs, nearly breaking Rosalind's heart.

"Do not worry so, my lady. Ms. Rivers said she will watch over them and keep them well and happy until you see them again."

"Are you not going to be here?" Rosalind asked as she went to the jug and bowl and picked up a cloth to wash her face.

"I have been instructed to come with you as chaperone on the journey to London and to help in town until His Grace has secured a companion for you. But I shall remain as your maid—although I am not certain I meet the standards of a London lady maid—but I shall study the latest fashions and hair designs to ensure you are the prettiest debutante in town. I promise you that."

Rosalind smiled and sat down at her dressing table, picking up her brush and running it through her long, brown locks. "Thank you, Mary. Having you in town will no doubt help me with my homesickness, I am certain."

"I will do all I can to make that so, my lady."

Rosalind finished preparing for the day, making sure to pack her favorite books for the journey and some games that she might play with Mary or the duke if he were traveling with her in the carriage.

Her goodbyes to her sisters were bittersweet. As much as she did not wish to leave them, it was necessary for the sake of their future happiness.

The duke, quiet and distracted, stood near the carriage—his horse already saddled—so that she would be traveling on her own with her maid. A little stab of disappointment ran through her at the thought. She enjoyed his company and conversation, and though spending many hours with her maid was not unpleasant, it would ultimately result in her maid dozing off while Rosalind herself grew bored, waiting for them to reach their first stop for the night.

"Goodbye, my darlings. I shall write each week, I promise," she called out the carriage window as the vehicle started forward.

Her dear sisters' faces—with forced smiles as they waved goodbye—brought tears to her eyes. She leaned out the carriage window, watching them and waving until they could no longer be seen.

She sat back in the squabs and thanked her maid when a handkerchief was passed to her. Forcing herself to remember that it was not forever. That she would see them again and their parting wasn't final. They traveled all day, stopping only for luncheon on the side of the road. Rosalind cringed, feeling sorry for the duke as he opened the pie that the cook had made for them, a tasteless dry meal that she herself struggled to swallow.

The poor man would have to replace their old cook soon if he were to survive the coming winter at the estate. But at least Rosalind was assured that he would take care of their cook in her dotage.

Their first night was spent at the Whistle Inn, before rising early and traveling on at the break of dawn the following morning. They reached the outskirts of London by late the following afternoon.

Buoyed by the thought of seeing a city she had only ever dreamed of visiting, Rosalind rolled down the carriage window once again and leaned out, watching the streets pass by. Beyond the city limits were market gardens and small farms, but these soon gave way to numerous cottages and then to large stone buildings. Central Mayfair was a bustling hive of activity.

Numerous ladies and gentlemen strolled along the cobblestone and gravel streets, their footpaths paved with large flagstones. They made their way to Grosvenor Square—her father's London address, which she had only ever heard of in correspondence, but never seen.

The carriage pulled into a large, private drive and stopped before a monstrous Georgian mansion. Several footmen, along with household staff, came out to greet them, and Rosalind frowned, having never known that her father employed so many staff in town.

However had he afforded them all?

She climbed down with the help of the duke,

who came to her side, taking her hand and wrapping it about his arm.

"Are you ready for London, Lady Rosalind?" he asked.

She smiled, unable to hide her excitement. A better question would be: was London ready for her?

CHAPTER
EIGHT

L ady Rosalind smiled at the waiting staff and exchanged a few pleasantries before the housekeeper approached and introduced herself.

"I'm Mrs. Wilson, Your Grace, Lady Rosalind. And may we offer our condolences regarding your father—what a great loss it must be for you and your family, my lady."

"Thank you. You are very kind," Rosalind managed to reply, though she did not share such melancholy thoughts about her father. He had been cold and unforgiving toward his six daughters—blaming and even hating them simply for being the females they were born as and the ladies they had become. That the staff here appeared genuinely downcast over the duke's passing gave her a small measure of solace. Perhaps he had not been such a beast to them. Maybe he was happier in London, and the servants here were treated with greater kindness than those back home.

"Come, Your Grace, Lady Rosalind. I shall show you around the house before I guide you upstairs to your rooms."

"Thank you."

As they entered the foyer, the duke slipped Rosalind's arm free. The staff who had greeted them outside gradually returned to their duties, disappearing into the bustling corridors of the mansion.

Rosalind glanced upward at the two-story foyer, where a sweeping staircase flanked both sides of the upper floor. She had never seen anything so beautiful. She had never imagined that houses in London could rival the grandeur of their cousin country estates, yet the Ravensmere London estate appeared capable of matching even her beloved home in Hampshire.

The housekeeper led them through numerous rooms—the dining room, the billiard and drawing rooms, the duke's library, and even the private office adjoining his own, reserved for his future wife. Rosalind found herself especially taken with the latter, for in its refined quiet she could almost envision her dear mother seated behind a lady's desk or gazing out at the lush gardens that surrounded the home.

"The ballroom is upstairs along with the painting gallery and a private parlor for the lady of the house," the housekeeper explained as she guided them into a large room at the back of the mansion. "There is also a terrace through here. This room is east-facing, so it receives beautiful morning light. The late duke often broke his fast on the terrace when the weather permitted."

Rosalind offered the housekeeper a small smile, though she found little pleasure in discussing her father. He had despised them, and in turn, they had come to repudiate him. Whether he found solace on a terrace mattered little to her.

"There is a conservatory, where the duke— most fond of exotic fruits—kept banana and orange plants. There is, of course, a lovely seated area there as well if you desire a change of scenery."

"Sounds delightful. And what do the grounds of the property entail?" the duke inquired, catching Rosalind's eye as he followed the housekeeper into a back drawing room that overlooked the gardens.

"The mews lie at the rear of the grounds, and a tall stone wall encloses the property for security. There is a small pond with a fountain, and a large hedge runs along the wall to ensure privacy. The garden boasts several established trees and even a small wooden structure where one might sit outdoors and read. Jasmine has grown over it entirely, and it's a lovely cool position in the garden on a hot day. You are most welcome to explore if you wish before I show you to your rooms."

Rosalind shook her head. "No, thank you. I must freshen up—and perhaps take a short nap —before this evening's dinner."

"I have an appointment that cannot be postponed, so I shall not be in for dinner," the duke said, moving to leave.

"You're going out?" Rosalind blurted before she could stop herself. Sensing the awkwardness of the remark, the housekeeper curtsied and departed, likely to await their request for further guidance.

"I am," the duke replied. "I have some pressing business that requires my attention, so I shall dine with you another night."

"I hope there is nothing wrong, Your Grace?" Rosalind ventured, not yet ready to call him Nathaniel, even though he had given her leave. With the duke somewhat distracted at that moment, it did not seem the proper time for familiarity.

"Nothing at all. Merely a situation that requires my attention. I shall be back for breakfast."

"I shall see you in the morning then, Your Grace." Rosalind curtsied and made her way toward the front foyer, noting with a twinge of disappointment that no footsteps followed her.

The duke was, after all, a busy man—perhaps a matter concerning his ducal or earldom demanded his immediate input. There was no sign of any mistress, nor any suggestion that he had rushed back to London solely to be with her. Still, the thought left a sour taste in her mouth, and she composed herself when she next met the housekeeper in the foyer.

"Lady Rosalind, would you like me to take you to your room now?" the housekeeper asked.

"Please, thank you. And if you could arrange for some hot water and have my dinner served in my room this evening, that would be most helpful."

"Of course, my lady. Come," the housekeeper said as she led her up the stairs. "Your room is in the west wing and offers a lovely view of the back gardens. I think you shall like it very much."

"I'm certain I shall."

Rosalind loved her new suite of rooms. It was a far cry from the modest quarters of her late father's country estate. This room was opulent, clean, and bright. New linens adorned the bed—a pretty blue-and-white-floral pattern embroidered on the bedspread—and an abundance of pillows, along with two candlelit lamps on matching wooden side tables, lent an air of comfort. Rosalind strolled about, running her hand along the mahogany writing desk and the elegant dressing table, complete with a mirror positioned high enough to see her full reflection.

The curtains were drawn aside so that she could gaze out onto the yard. Outside, a gardener trimmed the roses while another meticulously tended the large hedge that bordered the property, ensuring that nothing was out of place.

Rosalind wondered silently. Was all this opulence provided by the new duke, or had her father reserved more funds for his London home than for his country estate? Could she even ask the duke such a question? Perhaps she was being overly suspicious of her late father. After all, he had given them no reason to believe that any of his words or actions held truth, despite the considerable money suggested by their surprisingly generous dowries. Why, then, would he allow his country seat to wither away without proper care? It made little sense—but then, her father had always been so bitter toward his family; perhaps he acted merely out of spite.

A knock at the door interrupted her musings. Her maid entered, directing the footmen to place the trunks in the dressing room adjoining her bedroom. Once they had departed, Rosalind stepped into the dressing room and peeked around the corner into the washroom—a small rectangular space equipped with a bath and towels, all arranged for her comfort.

"How lovely to have a private space apart

from the bedroom in which to bathe," she thought aloud. "I think I shall enjoy my time here. Who knew a house could offer so many luxuries?"

"Oh indeed, my lady," the maid replied. "But I believe some of the finer furnishings in these rooms are due to the new duke. I overheard a footman and a maid discussing it downstairs. He sent orders—and, from what I gathered, an abundance of funds—to ensure his arrival went smoothly and that nothing was amiss. This room's inviting state is evidence that his wishes were fulfilled."

"Indeed, the room is most pleasing." So it was not her papa who had been living an opulent lifestyle in London, but rather another kindness the new duke extended for her stay—and for her sisters when their debuts arrived. What a good and kind man he was.

Handsome, too.

CHAPTER
NINE

Rosalind sat in the drawing room that overlooked the terrace, having breakfasted alone that morning. There was no sign of the duke, even though he had promised the previous day that he would return to dine with her.

She flipped through the latest *La Belle Asemblée* and considered which type of dress in the current fashion publication might suit her. Taller than most women—a tall meg as she'd been termed by the reverend's son back home several years before—left her a little self-conscious of her height. Now, however, she regarded it as a blessing. The duke was tall. Surely His Grace would prefer a taller wife...

At the sound of voices and accompanying laughter, she straightened and turned toward the door just as it opened. In stepped Duke Ravensmere, accompanied by a woman whom she had never seen before.

Lady Rosalind rose, her mind racing to identify the newcomer. The woman exuded an air of superiority; her gown alone showcased the finest quality and the latest fashion throughout London this Season—much like the ones Rosalind had admired in her periodical.

"Lady Rosalind, may I present to you your companion for the Season. This is Lady Smithe, but you may call her Vivian." The duke turned toward the woman at his side, a small smile playing on his lips. "Of course, only if that is agreeable with you, my lady."

Lady Smithe clutched the duke's arm, her fingers tightening on his dark cloth jacket as she pressed even closer. Rosalind observed their interaction and wondered if there was something more than friendship between them. How well did the duke know this woman? She noted that Lady Smithe was undoubtedly attractive, with a curvy, distinctly feminine figure, and her smile directed at the duke was undeniably pretty.

Rosalind swallowed a surge of jealousy that swept over her as she compared herself to them both. Her own gown was several years out of fashion and far too small—especially around the bust. She silently cursed her father for his inability to care for them and leave them in such a poor state of well-being.

"It's lovely to meet you, Lady Smithe. Thank you for offering to guide me through my Season."

Lady Smithe brushed aside Rosalind's greeting without meeting her eyes, continuing instead to gaze adoringly at the duke. "It is no bother. I'm here for the Season in any case. When His Grace asked for my help, how could I refuse?"

Rosalind nodded. "Would you care to sit so we may get to know each other better?"

The duke led Lady Smithe over to a nearby settee where they both took a seat. "How do you know each other, if I may ask?" Rosalind inquired as she leaned back in her chair, clasping the publication close to her chest—a protective gesture born of uncertainty of the lady before her.

"My sister, the Countess of Ghent, married Ravensmere's best friend the earl, and so we've been thrown into each other's social spheres for several years now."

"How lovely." Rosalind paused, uncertain of her own feelings regarding their friendship—a question she resolved to mull over later. For now, she needed to learn more about her Season and what it would entail with Lady Smithe as her companion.

"So, I have never had a Season, which I'm sure the duke mentioned. Will you collect me each day for the events we're to attend? Or will you reside here? I assume the former, as you're married, and I should not think your husband would wish you far from his side."

Lady Smithe laughed, her hand scandalously clasping the duke's thigh. Rosalind looked away from the unexpected contact, now more convinced than ever that there was something between the pair.

"Oh, no, you are all wrong, Lady Rosalind. I'm a widow and therefore I shall move into the ducal home here with you, and we shall go about the Season under one roof. It makes much more sense, I believe, to do it this way. We shall be so very busy—with fittings for your gowns, purchasing new shoes and hats, gloves, jewelery. You shall be the Diamond of the Season after I have finished buffing you up like a sparkling jewel."

The idea sounded wonderful, and Rosalind hoped she would prove to be a success.

"May I ask, how old are you, my dear?" Lady Smithe inquired, her gaze taking in Rosalind's tattered gown for the first time since they sat.

"I'm three-and-twenty, my lady."

"Oh, my heavens. So you are my age. Well, I'm certain we shall get along very well."

Rosalind felt conflicted. The woman before her—smart, confident, attractive, and forthright —had already been married and was now a wealthy widow. This fact did nothing to bolster Rosalind's self-esteem, nor did she truly believe that they would be friends. The woman's words, while hopeful and kind, held a timbre of mockery to them.

"Had I been afforded a Season before this year, I'm certain we would have been friends." And had her father not died, perhaps she and her sisters might still be languishing in the country until they were well past the age to marry, a fate unthinkable for her siblings, who were kind and beautiful young women. If only their dearest mama had outlived their father...

"I have organized a carriage for you both to-day, and Lady Smithe has instructed her maid to pack her things and move into the house. This afternoon, you will go shopping and begin prepa-rations for the forthcoming Season. I promised Lady Rosalind that I would find her a loving hus-band, and that is what I shall do."

"You are too kind, dearest duke," Lady Smithe remarked, once again leaning over His Grace in a manner Rosalind found far too familiar. The woman would soon be sitting on the duke's lap if she moved any closer.

"Thank you, Your Grace. I do hope you're right."

Later that afternoon, as arranged by the duke, a carriage pulled up outside the London townhouse to take Rosalind and Lady Smithe shopping on Bond Street. Within minutes, they were gliding along the busy thorough-fare toward a well-regarded modiste.

Inside the shop, a team of assistants presented an array of colored muslin and silks—various cuts and fabrics from which Rosalind could choose.

"I'm dark-haired, and a touch of the sun has warmed my complexion," Rosalind observed. "I believe a darker shade of gown would suit me best—no pastels."

"You are right," Madame Leroy replied, her thick French accent lending a refined lilt to her words. "You shall look beautiful in reds and blues, and a green riding suit would be ideal, I believe."

"Do you truly think so?" Lady Smithe interjected, frowning at the vibrant colors displayed before them. "You are a debutante, after all, and you should not be in bright, rich hues. It would be better to choose shades in pastels—they would suit you much more."

The modiste met Rosalind's eye and offered the slightest shake of her head, silently conveying her own preference without words.

"Thank you for your opinion, Lady Smithe. I shall defer to it on many things as you guide me through the Season, but I cannot wear colors that are pale and washed out. I must make an impression if I am to attract a husband—the gentlemen this year will not notice a wallflower. I want to shine, and on this occasion, I shall choose the colors that suit me best."

Lady Smithe's lips pursed into a displeased line, and Rosalind silently hoped she had not offended her. Despite her own insecurities, Rosalind wished for genuine friendship between them.

"Very good, Lady Rosalind," Madame Leroy announced as she moved to a nearby cupboard. She retrieved several large leather-bound volumes and set them on the table. "These are the cuts and styles of gowns available this year. Browse through them, and we shall select several dresses to prepare you for the Season. More can be made as the Season progresses."

"Thank you," Rosalind breathed, barely able to contain her excitement. The prospect of acquiring new gowns thrilled her—a welcome change from the dowdy dresses that had been too small or too short, constantly mended over the years. With eager anticipation, she prepared to open the tome and choose the designs that would usher her into a bold new future.

CHAPTER
TEN

Nathaniel rose and shook his steward Malcolm's hand before gesturing for him to sit. He had not seen Malcolm for several weeks, but now that he was back in London, his steward had urgent news that could not wait.

"Malcolm, it's good to see you. What is it that's had me return from the country with such urgency?"

"Your Grace, it is good that you're back. However, this matter could not wait, and because of its delicate nature, I could not simply send the information by correspondence. I had to see you in person to avoid any miscommunication."

Malcolm's harried countenance put Nathaniel on guard, so he gave his full attention. "Tell me what has happened, and we shall discuss the matter."

"Of course, Your Grace." Malcolm slid several papers across the table. "I have discovered, now that you're at Ravensmere, that the late duke maintained a long-term mistress in town—a woman he began seeing not long after his wife, the duchess, passed away. It has come to my attention that she lived here with the duke, unbeknownst to society. But that is not all I have uncovered."

Nathaniel rifled through the documents, noting several birth certificates. "What is all this?"

"Well, Your Grace, the duke had three daughters by his mistress. From what I can ascertain, the eldest is just eighteen, with the other two being fourteen-year-old twins. They now reside in Cheapside, where the duke purchased a house for them. Contrary to rumor, the duke was fond of the mistress and the daughters she bore him—unlike his legitimate children, one of whom is now in town for the Season."

The revelation troubled Nathaniel deeply. Lady Rosalind—a diamond if ever he had seen one—risked having her debut into society ruined if this scandal became public. How could she ever enter society knowing her father had borne three children out of wedlock? Their unforgiving society would taint not only her reputation but also that of her sisters.

"We must not utter a word of this to anyone,"

Nathaniel instructed. "Keep it between us until we know if the mistress intends to seek further monetary compensation as the duke's lover. If he purchased them a house, there is a good chance he left them a stipend in his will, though I do not recall that being mentioned during the reading."

"That is precisely the issue, Your Grace. I spoke to the late duke's solicitor, and it appears he essentially had two parts to his will—one to be read out before his legitimate children and one for his illegitimate ones." Malcolm paused. "In effect, he ordered that only certain sections of his will be read to each branch of his family. The man was truly despicable."

"So Lady Rosalind and her sisters remain unaware of the others living here in London?"

"I do believe that is the case, Your Grace."

"And what of the illegitimate siblings? They must know the duke had another family in the country, and that he was a widower. Do you believe the mistress will cause any trouble for Lady Rosalind and her sisters during the Season or in the future?"

"That I cannot say, Your Grace, though I hope not. Perhaps we might consider offering a sum that would keep the mistress satisfied and quiet while Lady Rosalind finds a husband. Not that she will necessarily seek an audience with you, but we must be prepared should she do so."

"I think that is a prudent idea. I shall contemplate a sum and have it ready in case we need to act swiftly. One never knows what past lovers are capable of, especially if they believe their daughters have been slighted."

A pause fell over the room before Malcolm continued. "There is also a rumor among the household that the opulence of the house is being attributed to you, Your Grace. Many of the staff here are new—aside from the butler and housekeeper. They all left when the duke passed, uncertain of their future employment. But those who have been hired since are crediting the refurbishment of the home to your patronage."

"And why is that a concern? Let them believe what they will." Nathaniel regarded it as trivial. It mattered little who had refurbished the house.

"However, Lady Rosalind now believes that the advancements to the living arrangements were at your expense, which is not the case. They were ordered by the late duke, who wanted his mistress and the daughters she bore to live in luxury—luxury he believed they deserved."

Nathaniel absorbed these words, recalling the shabby state of the country estate: tattered window coverings, worn rugs, and cobwebbed, unused rooms. As for the children's clothing, the duke had done them no favors by allowing them to live in squalor. If Lady Rosalind discovered that her father despised them even more than she suspected, her heart would surely break.

"The room that Lady Rosalind occupies upstairs—whose room was it before the duke's passing? I must know where the late duke placed his priorities."

"That was the room of his eldest illegitimate daughter. Blue was her favorite color—and from what I have learned, it was also the duke's."

Nathaniel leaned back, rubbing his jaw as stubble prickled his palm. A deep sadness gripped him; the duke's daughters deserved far better. How sorry he felt for them all.

The front door opened and voices sounded in the foyer. Through his office, Nathaniel watched Lady Rosalind and Lady Smithe enter, accompanied by several footmen bearing numerous boxes from their shopping. He stood and strode from his room, smiling as he noted the bounty of purchases Lady Rosalind had made for the Season.

"Oh, Your Grace, so good of you to come see. Look at everything we have purchased for our dearest Lady Rosalind." Lady Smithe gestured toward the many boxes—too many to count.

"So your first shopping expedition was a success, it seems. Did you manage to acquire everything you hoped for to commence the Season?"

Lady Rosalind offered a quiet nod and a pleasant smile. "I believe so, Your Grace. Thank you again for attending to my needs." She curtsied briefly. "If you'll excuse me, I must write letters to my sisters. I wish for the missives to be sent today."

Lady Smithe stepped beside Nathaniel. "Of course, my dear. I shall see you at luncheon."

"Very good," Lady Rosalind replied as she ascended the stairs.

Nathaniel watched her for a moment, unease pricking his spine. "Is everything well between you and Lady Rosalind? I thought she would be far happier with her purchases today than she appears."

Lady Smithe sighed, concern etched on her features. "I suggested, during the selection of materials for her new gowns, that she choose colors more suited to a debutante. I fear I may have hurt her feelings. Lady Rosalind desired richer hues, but I overruled her, opting for pastels instead. I worry I have disappointed her."

Pastel-colored dresses might seem appropriate, yet Nathaniel believed they would not flatter his ward. With her dark hair and sun-kissed complexion, the deeper shades would suit better. They would bring out the colour of her eyes. She was a striking woman, and those tones would enhance her natural beauty, even he as a man knew that much.

"And so Lady Rosalind is upset?" he observed, disliking the thought Rosalind feeling disheartened on what should be a joyous, liberating occasion.

"Yes, she is, but trust that I have her best interests at heart, Your Grace."

Nathaniel hoped fervently that this was true. "Of course. I never doubted you."

CHAPTER
ELEVEN

A letter arrived later that afternoon, and after what should have been an exciting day of shopping—compounded by a missive from her sisters—Rosalind found herself steeped in melancholy. She had eagerly anticipated the Season, dreaming of finding a gentleman whose character and beliefs aligned with her own. Now, however, she doubted that anyone would be attracted to her.

The gowns, though cut in the latest fashion, came in dreadful hues that left her looking washed out and sickly. No matter how much she tried to persuade Lady Smithe that she knew what would suit her best, her ladyship refused to alter the directive, firmly convinced that her choices were ideal and Rosalind's were not.

Seeking solitude, Rosalind slipped away beneath a weeping willow, hiding from the staff and the duke should anyone be searching for her.

She could not bear to let anyone see her so distraught. The prospect of Lady Smithe moving in with them only added to her dismay—a woman of such refined taste should have agreed that pastels were entirely unsuited to her complexion. Why insist on such hideous colors?

"Rosalind, is that you in there?"

The deep timbre of the duke's voice startled her from her sulky reverie. "Yes, it's me. I thought I'd take a turn about the gardens before dinner."

The duke ducked beneath the low-hanging branches and joined her. "I thought I saw you leave the terrace, and since Lady Smithe is not here until tomorrow, I assumed you had escaped the house for a quiet moment." He paused, watching her closely. Did he sense the absence of her usual cheer?

"What is wrong?" he inquired as he guided her to an iron bench at the base of the tree. Once seated, he took her hand, his thumb idly rubbing the tops of her fingers. "You have not been yourself since you returned from shopping. Was the day not as you had hoped?"

Rosalind could not bring herself to lie. They had become friends, and he had done so much for her. Torn between obligation and despair, she felt compelled to confess her disappointment.

"As much as I love the dresses ordered today, they are not to my liking. I do not suit the pastel colors that Lady Smithe insists are best. I am three-and-twenty—barely much younger than you—yet I am expected to dress like a child for my debut. It makes no sense, and I am deeply disappointed."

The duke's gaze softened. "No matter what you wear, Rosalind, few men would fail to see you as the diamond that you are. You are personable and, though I ought not to say this as your guardian, utterly breathtaking. Men will flock to you, whether you are clad in pastel pink or royal blue."

Rosalind's vision blurred at his sweet words. He was so kind and handsome, and her stomach knotted when he gently wiped away a tear from her cheek before cupping her face. She could not tear her gaze away as he watched her intently, his head lowered toward hers. The thought that she might receive her first kiss from the man she had come to admire seemed like a dream come true. Yet she knew she should not—it was his duty as her guardian, and she, his ward, to be guided through the Season.

Still, Rosalind moistened her dry lips and leaned toward him, suddenly aware that her hand had reached for him, clutching the lapels of his superfine coat. "You're so beautiful. You will be swept off your feet and proposed to before you can do anything to stop it."

She nodded, though the thought of marriage at that moment mattered little. All she desired was to kiss the man before her—a man who made her stomach lurch, her skin tingle, and sent heat pooling between her legs in a way she had never experienced. She longed for that rush every time she was with a man, yet she knew that from this night forward, it would only be with the duke.

His hand slipped low along her jaw as he tipped her face upward to meet his. "Tell me to stop, Rosalind. I ache to kiss you, and I should not."

"Why should you not? We are not so far apart in age as to make it wrong. You are only three years older. A kiss does not hurt anyone, does it?"

"I'm your guardian." He pressed his forehead against hers, resisting the urge that pulsed between them like an invisible shield.

"I do not care who you are, but if you do not kiss me here and now under this willow tree, I shall cease to exist."

His mouth curved into a mischievous grin as she tightened her grip on him, pulling him closer. "Kiss me, Duke. Be my first if you're determined not to be my last."

He growled, his eyes darkening with hunger, and shattered the barrier between them with a kiss. At first, his lips brushed hers softly and beckoned. Rosalind reveled in their tender contact—his soft, eager kiss urging her to follow his lead, to plunge headlong into the unknown and savor the fall. She parted her lips for him, yielding to the kiss as they both desired. His tongue teased hers, and she moaned, unable to stifle the sound. His kiss sent a surge of desire coursing through her veins, and she pressed closer, yearning for more, longing to feel his hands beyond just her cheek.

He pulled her into his arms, and all tenderness gave way as the kiss grew wild, hungry, and wanton. Rosalind tried to match the urgency of Nathaniel's kiss, but her mind whirled and her body burned with craving. She wanted more—so much more.

His kisses trailed down her jaw and neck. He playfully bite on her earlobe, making her shiver. "You're wicked, Nathaniel."

His rumbling laugh carried a warning she should heed, but she ignored it. "You have no idea, Rosalind." He paused, kissing the hollow of her neck before moving along her shoulder blade. His hand slid over her breast, and she pressed farther into his embrace. He kneaded her there, his thumb and forefinger teasing her nipple beneath her gown. A jolt of sensation shot to her core, and she crossed her legs in a futile attempt to ease the ache he provoked.

"Of all the things I want to do to you—I am a scoundrel, a rake who ought to be shot for kissing you now. You should stop me."

"I do not want to stop you. Quite the opposite, in fact." She clasped his jaw and pulled him back for another kiss, needing to feel him, to revel in his wild, wanton kisses that made her feel so alive. For the first time in her life, she felt truly alive—loved and desired.

"Your kisses are wicked."

"They are, and I should not be doing this. We should not be doing this." He broke free from her hold and stood, pacing on the bench before her. Running a hand through his tousled hair, he appeared even more handsome—disheveled, as if he had been kissed to the very edge of his life. She hoped she had had the same effect on him.

Rosalind felt transformed, as if her life had suddenly opened to new possibilities and experiences she longed to explore.

"And if I desire more of these kisses in the garden, will you relent and give me what I want?"

He stared at her, his gaze falling to her lips. She watched him, hoping he could read the desire written on her face.

"You're my ward. I am only here to guide you through the Season, nothing more."

"I have Lady Smithe for that."

"Do not be a teasing minx. It does not suit you."

She shrugged, unconcerned by his admonition. "You may be wrong, Your Grace. Perhaps it does suit me very well."

CHAPTER
TWELVE

Nathaniel paced, his mind tormented by Rosalind's parting look—a gaze that promised more, even as his duty demanded restraint. Her lips, still swollen from his previous kisses, and her cheeks, flushed with lingering desire, beckoned him to cast aside all caution. Yet he could not indulge that temptation again.

"I'm sorry, Rosalind, but we cannot do this again. I take full responsibility for my lapse in decorum and restraint. Please forgive me. Good night."

With that, he left her beneath the sheltering branches, each step toward the house weighted by the knowledge that he must not stray from the path of propriety. He was her guardian, expected to guide and protect, not to succumb to his carnal urges—even if those urges threatened to overwhelm him.

As he climbed the terrace stairs, Nathaniel adjusted his breeches, painfully aware of the throbbing evidence of his desire. The sanctuary of his bedroom in the newly assembled ducal Mayfair home offered a temporary refuge. He closed and locked the door behind him, comforted by the silence and shadow of the room, where heavy curtains and a pair of flickering candles cast dancing shapes on the walls.

Nathaniel stripped his clothing with hurried resolve, desperate to release the tension pulsing through him. Though he could have sought escape in the arms of a courtesan at a nearby establishment, the memory of Rosalind's soft lips and lingering warmth haunted him too vividly. Instead, he stood before the roaring fire, his mind a tempest of forbidden thoughts. His hand found its way to his aroused member, and he allowed himself a brief, illicit indulgence—imagining Rosalind on her knees before him, her delicate mouth and teasing tongue driving him to the brink.

The fantasy was as vivid as it was damning; he moaned softly as he worked himself over, the image of her beauty and desire mingling with the heat of the flames until he finally released his pent-up need. For several long minutes, he stood there, caught between shame and longing, before finally striding to the washbasin to cleanse himself of the evidence of his weakness.

His bed beckoned. Clad only in the vulnerability of his naked skin—a habit borne of the sweltering summers of his youth—he climbed in, though even now his thoughts betrayed him. The image of Rosalind joining him in his bed sent a shiver of anticipation through his body, a forbidden thrill he knew he must never allow to come to fruition.

N athaniel managed to avoid Rosalind until the following afternoon. When she returned from her shopping expedition with Lady Smithe, he was already heading out to his club, eager to escape the oppressive scent of jasmine that clung to his clothes—a haunting reminder of their stolen moment beneath the willow.

"Your Grace, are you heading out? We were hoping to dine with you this evening, for it is my first night living here with you all. What a jolly good time we shall have this Season. I do not believe I have ever been so excited, not even at my own debut." Lady Smithe's voice rang out, cheerful and bright, between Rosalind and him. But Nathaniel's heart was heavy. The presence of Lady Smithe under the same roof meant fewer moments alone with Rosalind—a thought that should have been a comfort, but instead filled him with a deep, bitter regret.

He forced his gaze away from Rosalind's

pretty blue eyes, which seemed to hold an un-spoken longing he dared not meet. The promise he had made to himself—that she was off limits —echoed in his mind.

"Unfortunately, I am much engaged until the Season itself, but I will, of course, escort you both to Lord and Lady Coke's ball," he announced.

"Should we not host our own coming-out ball for Rosalind before the Season starts in earnest?" Lady Smithe suggested, her tone light yet insistent. "It is only proper. We can invite the most influential and upstanding gentlemen, en-suring that she makes a fine match without delay."

"I will not choose a husband for Lady Ros-alind without first knowing her req—" he began.

"Yes, yes," Lady Smithe interrupted, turning toward Rosalind. "Of course, dear, you shall have final say in the match, but the men at your ball will be eligible, rich, and suitable for a duke's daughter—even if you are a bit coarse around the edges. With some guidance, you'll shine like a star in the night sky, not lost like so many other wallflowers."

Nathaniel regarded Lady Smithe uncertainly. Though Rosalind might be less polished than some, she was far from foolish. She was intelli-gent enough to navigate high society's subtle cues. Her beauty and the generous dowry he had arranged for her and her sisters made him confident in her prospects, even if the fickle *ton* valued a pretty face above all else.

Still, he could not meet Rosalind's eyes, fearful that their shared longing might unravel the resolve he had so painstakingly forged.

"We can host a coming-out ball, certainly. Make the arrangements, Lady Smithe." Taking his greatcoat and hat from a waiting footman, he prepared to depart. "Good day to you both."

But as he reached the threshold, his gaze slipped to Rosalind. Her delicate features struck him like a blow—her eyes, filled with longing and hope, nearly shattered his determination. For a brief, agonizing moment, he longed to rush to her, to pull her into his arms and kiss her once more. To see for himself if what they had shared under the willow was real.

"What a wonderful day this has turned out to be—a ball to prepare for. I shall be even busier, organizing invitations posthaste," Lady Smithe declared as she ascended the stairs with Rosalind following, though not without casting a final, lingering glance in his direction.

Nathaniel forced himself away, leaving for his club and the relative anonymity of the upstairs brandy room at Whites. There, he slumped into a leather chair, looking out over St. James Street as conversations of gentlemen drifted around him. A footman soon served him a glass of brandy, which he sipped slowly to fortify his resolve as he wallowed in the torment of his own making.

"Ravensmere!" The voice of his good friend, Cameron—the Marquess of Issacs—broke through his brooding silence. The marquess joined him, gesturing for a refill of his own whisky glass.

"May I be one of the first to congratulate you on your windfall? A ducal title does not come about every day," his friend said warmly.

Nathaniel raised his glass in salute. "I thank you, my friend, but it is not without its troubles."

Lord Issacs chuckled, settling back in his chair. "What hardship can there be when one inherits one of the prettiest country estates in England and one of the grandest London homes ever built?"

All of that was true, yet nothing compared to the personal trouble that had seized Nathaniel's thoughts since yesterday afternoon.

"The estate came with six wards. I find myself guardian to six women, each requiring a Season. I fear I shall be an old man before I have them all married."

The marquess whistled and laughed. "Are any of them pretty?"

Nathaniel shook his head. "Pretty? One is breathtakingly beautiful and kind. A most troubling pairing." He sighed, knowing that despite his best intentions, the complexities of duty and desire would weigh on him long into the coming days.

Even when the brandy warmed his veins, he wondered whether any man could truly escape the pull of passion. He inwardly cursed, knowing the truth to that answer. He was doomed for failure.

THIRTEEN

Over the following days, too many to count, Rosalind rarely saw the duke. Whenever she caught even a glimpse of him about the house, he averted his gaze—ducking into his office or slipping out the door. The warm camaraderie that had begun to form before their passionate kiss beneath the willow tree had receded into a distant, bittersweet memory.

How she regretted that kiss. She longed instead for his friendship, for the gentle, encouraging words that had once promised guidance for the Season and her coming-out ball—a ball that had taken on a life of its own, thanks largely to Lady Smithe. More than anything, Rosalind missed their conversations. She needed to speak to him, to assure him that she would never again risk such a transgression, and to beg that he restore their friendship. After all, he was her guardian, her only link to family here in London, and in that role, she required him now more than ever.

Rosalind sat before her dressing table mirror preparing for her coming-out ball. She beheld the vision her maid had crafted—for a debut that would herald her entry into the society destined to shape her life. The reflection that met her eyes was almost unrecognizable. Once, she had been the country daughter of a duke, clad in garments a size too small and gowns that were years out of fashion. A girl who wore nothing but a simple ribbon to hold up her hair.

Now, however, the woman staring back was a stranger—a refined creation molded to society's exacting standards. The gown, a sumptuous, rich pink that defied any notion of pastels, transformed her entirely. In that moment, she silently resolved to thank Lady Smithe for her change of heart regarding the dress. When her maid had first revealed the gown, Rosalind could scarcely believe her eyes, recalling how she had been expected to wear a washed-out color. But this dress —with its empire-cut bodice, delicate puffy sleeves resting gracefully on her shoulders, and a fit that accentuated curves she had never imagined were hers—made her question who she truly was.

A soft voice from behind the mirror declared, "You look utterly beautiful, Lady Rosalind. There will not be a gentleman present who will not fall at your feet—so lovely you are this evening." Her maid, having secured the final diamond pin into Rosalind's hair, stepped back with a proud smile. "I do believe I have surpassed myself tonight. How delightful you look, my lady."

Rosalind returned the smile. "Thank you, Mary. You have exceeded my expectations. I do not know how to thank you enough."

With a gentle laugh, the maid waved away the compliment. "It is my pleasure. I only wish for your and your sisters' happiness—you deserve nothing less."

The door to her room swung open, and in strolled Lady Smithe, resplendent in a gown of royal-blue silk and an exquisite headpiece adorned with a single, artful feather—a statement few could miss.

Her steps faltered, and the smile on her face vanished as she took in Rosalind's gown. "Whatever are you wearing? That is not the gown that was ordered for this evening!" Lady Smithe strode over, forcibly pulling Rosalind from her seat. She inspected the gown as though it were a repugnant creature in need of extermination. "You must change. This is not what we ordered." Her tone was low and menacing. For a moment, Rosalind braced herself for her ladyship to stomp her slippered foot. "I shall have words with the dressmaker. How dare she go against my wishes and produce something so utterly unacceptable —I will have the duke refuse to pay for it."

Rosalind reached out, pleading, "Oh, please do not do that, Lady Smithe." Her touch was brusquely brushed aside. "I love this dress so very much, my lady. I thought that you changed your opinion on what I was to wear..." She paused, unsure of what she should say or do. "As I am already dressed, right down to my shoes, and the ball is about to start, perhaps I can stay clothed as I am. If I were to change now, I would be late to my own coming-out ball. Besides, this is the only gown delivered today. I have nothing else to wear."

With little patience for protest, Lady Smithe grumbled under her breath. "You there," she said to Rosalind's maid. "Go to my wardrobe and choose the most suitable gown for a debutante— a gown in pastel hues. Now, go!"

All hope for a successful evening evaporated as Lady Smithe seized Rosalind by the shoulders, forcibly turning her about and unfastening the gown at the back. "I cannot believe the dress-maker has betrayed me so! You look positively disheveled in this gown. What will people think if they see you in public in such an unsightly color?" she snapped.

Tears blurred Rosalind's vision, before she assisted in pushing the gown from her person, watching as it was thrown carelessly onto the bed like a piece of soiled cloth. "I don't believe the dress is so terrible for a debutante. Perhaps the modiste simply forgot the conversation regarding altering the colors." The last thing Rosalind wanted was for the modiste to be injured by Lady Smithe's ire.

Lady Smithe, however, was unyielding. "I shall have her head and her business before tomorrow's close for this error."

Rosalind inwardly wilted like the wallflower she had hoped not to become when her maid returned with a pastel-peach gown—a design from last year marred by a hideous stain near the bodice. "I cannot wear that, Lady Smithe. There is a stain on the muslin—do you not see it? I will be ridiculed in society for debuting in such a gown."

Lady Smithe dismissed her concerns with a curt wave. "Do not be ridiculous, Rosalind. The dress will do perfectly well."

With no alternative, Rosalind stepped into the dress and, with her maid's help, pulled it over her undergarments. When she caught her reflection in the mirror, despair threatened to overwhelm her. The hopeful image of her debut vanished, replaced by a vision of a colorless orphan in need of nourishment and sunlight. Yet, as her maid fastened the gown at the back and ensured every detail was in order, Rosalind rallied her resolve.

The duke had spared no expense for her coming-out ball—even if he no longer spoke to her as he once had—every requirement specified by Lady Smithe for the night had been met.

"There now, that is much better and entirely age-appropriate," her ladyship declared.

Rosalind narrowed her eyes, disliking that her ladyship continued to remark about her age. "We are both three-and-twenty, my lady, and you are wearing a gown of royal blue. I do not think what I was wearing would have caused any raised brows."

Lady Smithe snapped, "Tsk, tsk, tsk, my dear. We shall have no sulking. I am far more versed in the art of society than you, even those deemed past their prime." With a final, unfriendly smile, she added, "Now come, we must make your debut downstairs. The guests will be arriving soon."

With a heavy heart and trembling resolve, Rosalind followed Lady Smithe out of her room and toward the stairs.

Her stomach twisted as she descended, for her eyes caught sight of the duke. He stood with his back turned, engaged in conversation with an unfamiliar gentleman—an early arriving guest, perhaps. His strong back and broad shoulders set her heart fluttering, and she clenched her fists at her sides, fighting the impulse to reach out to him. Since that fateful kiss beneath the willow—

a kiss that had awakened in her a longing so intense she could not forget its sweetness—she had tasted the possibility of love. And she had adored it. Yet now, steeling her features against his habitual curt responses, she prepared herself for the cold indifference that had replaced their once-warm exchanges.

The duke turned as Lady Smithe joined him, and after a few words exchanged between them, his gaze met Rosalind's. In that moment, her breath caught, her skin prickled. However was she to remain indifferent to him? An impossible battle she would lose.

A frown creased his brow as his attention drifted to scrutinize her gown. Rosalind swallowed her disappointment. If the duke could barely conceal his disdain for her dress, few others would refrain from doing so. The night, already fraught with insecurity, seemed doomed to failure—and now, she was certain of it.

FOURTEEN

That dress was certainly not what he had ordered from the modiste for Lady Rosalind.

Nathaniel could not tear his gaze away from the atrocious gown that clung to her form. The peach frock did nothing for her complexion. In fact, it failed to bring out the luminous blue of her eyes and, somehow, rendered her pallid and sickly—an appearance utterly unbefitting the vibrant young woman she truly was.

Rosalind offered a polite smile as she approached him and Lord Issacs, who had arrived early—perhaps seeking the best seat in the room to avoid the prying matchmakers. She dipped into a curtsy, and Nathaniel could see the nervous tension in her stance. Was her apprehension born of the memory of their ill-advised kiss beneath the willow, or did she sense his own discontent with the gown?

"You look beautiful, Lady Rosalind. Are you ready to face the *ton*?" Nathaniel inquired, extending his arm to lead her into the ballroom.

"Of course, thank you, Your Grace. For everything."

Her voice was soft, but Nathaniel longed to ask more—why she wasn't wearing one of her new gowns, why this dress left her so vulnerable. Over the past days, he had craved every opportunity to be near her, each glimpse of her a refreshing draught after a long, arduous ride.

Yet duty constrained him. He was her guardian, and he had spared no expense to ensure only gentlemen of impeccable character and wealth attended her coming-out ball. He needed her to be happy and secure—even if it meant keeping himself at a distance, away from any temptation that might compel him to corner her in a dark room and test whether the spark from their kiss could ignite an uncontrollable blaze. He suspected it could.

They entered the ballroom, and within the hour, hundreds of guests gathered, each offering felicitations for a successful Season. Rosalind bore the burdens of her role as hostess with grace, but it was not long before Lord Felton—a refined earl from Kent, whom Nathaniel had high hopes for as a prospective suitor for Rosalind—whisked her away to dance. Lord Felton was of a mature age, wealthy and, by many accounts, handsome—a gentleman whose love of the countryside Nathaniel believed might appeal to her sensibilities.

As Nathaniel watched Lord Felton sweep Rosalind about the ballroom floor, he felt the intrusive warmth of Lady Smithe's hand slip about his arm. Her eyes, calculating and sharp, tracked Rosalind as though the young debutante were her own prized possession. Nathaniel, aware that neither Lady Smithe nor Rosalind was his wife, discreetly extricated himself from Lady Smithe's grasp, placing a measured distance between them.

"The gown isn't what I expected Lady Rosalind would be wearing this evening," he murmured darkly as he observed the scene. "This one is stained, and its color flatters her not at all." His eyes followed Rosalind and for the life of him he could not look away. A footman passed with a tray of wine, and he accepted a glass, downing a much-needed sip as he watched her laugh and converse with her gentleman admirer.

"Oh yes, there was a mistake at the modiste. I ordered a pastel-lilac ballgown, yet they delivered a gown of the deepest pink I've ever seen. I made Rosalind change before we came down— she cannot be seen in such a risqué color. Her Season would be over before it even began."

Annoyance thrummed through Nathaniel as he finished his drink and set it upon a nearby mantel. "So whose gown is that she is wearing? It barely fits her frame, and it is stained! Whoever deemed that gown appropriate must be held accountable." He cast a pointed glance toward Lady Smithe, noting with a grim satisfaction that her expression was contrite. He knew full well who had forced the change that left Rosalind in this unsuitable dress. Lady Smithe, it appeared, was not proving to be the best companion for his ward.

"It is only a small stain, Your Grace," she defended softly. "No one will pay much heed to it. Lady Rosalind is both pretty and personable— the men will favor engaging conversation over anything regarding her attire for the night."

Nathaniel raised his brows, unconvinced, yet unwilling to let Lady Smithe spoil Rosalind's coming-out ball or Season. "I will send word to the modiste that henceforth the gowns must be made in the colors chosen by Lady Rosalind. She is three-and-twenty. We cannot treat her as if she were a child of eighteen. Do not defy my wishes a second time, my lady, or I shall be forced to replace you as her companion for the remainder of the Season."

"Oh no, Your Grace," Lady Smithe replied, her tone edged with frustration. "The dress from the modiste did not fit well across the bust, and I had to secure another for her in haste. While I may not entirely agree with allowing Lady Rosalind to choose her own colors for a debutante's gown, I will, of course, abide by your rules. Whatever dresses are delivered over the coming days shall be worn, you can be assured of that."

"I do hope so," Nathaniel murmured bitterly. "For the gown she wears this evening seems designed to ruin her chances."

Lady Smithe's eyes widened, her cheeks flushing as Nathaniel's words cut deep. He knew then that her actions had been deliberate—a calculated act meant to undermine Rosalind. "She's too beautiful to have her prospects ruined," Lady Smithe countered dismissively, though she avoided his gaze. "Look at her in Lord Felton's arms—they seem to float in perfect harmony. I dare say it will only be a matter of weeks before she is whisked away on a proposal, removed from the marriage market."

A chill ran down Nathaniel's spine at the thought. He rolled his shoulders, disturbed by the idea of Rosalind, his cherished ward, being married off and living in another man's home— whether in London or the countryside. The notion of her warming another man's bed turned his stomach. "I will not rush Lady Rosalind, nor will you," he declared firmly. "She is to choose for herself when she finds a gentleman who loves her as dearly as she deserves."

"Oh, of course, Your Grace. I would not wish anything less for our dearest charge," Lady

Smithe replied, her tone sugary but insincere in Nathaniel's ears. He debated inwardly whether he should have hired her for the Season. Recently widowed, Lady Smithe seemed perfect for a companion. Yet now her behavior struck him as unnervingly spiteful. There was something in her manner around Rosalind that set his nerves on edge.

As the dance ended, Lord Felton returned Rosalind to his side. She offered his lordship a perfect curtsy. But before the next set began, Nathaniel reached for Rosalind's hand and pulled her onto the ballroom floor. She slipped into his arms as naturally as if they were meant to be, and for a fleeting moment, his mind was bombarded with the memory of their kiss. He drank in the sight of her—even in the ghastly, stained gown, she remained one of the most beautiful women he had ever beheld.

"Did you enjoy your dance with Lord Felton? Is he a contender for your heart?" he asked in a low, measured tone as he led her about the floor.

A soft, musical laugh escaped her. "Possibly —he is very kind, and he loves the country as much as I do. We might indeed be well matched in that regard." Her eyes sparkled, and as Nathaniel's gaze traveled appreciatively over her form—lingering on the gentle swell of her bosom and the graceful curve of her neck—he felt a familiar ache stir within him.

"I'm sorry about the dress," he continued, his tone tender yet resolute. "I will send word to the modiste that henceforth, no pastel shall be made for you. You are three-and-twenty, and you deserve to shine in colors that suit you, not ones that wash you out."

"Will you truly do that for me?" Her smile broadened with relief. "That is very sweet of you, Your Grace."

Though his words were kind, Nathaniel's heart harbored a storm of conflicted desire—a dark, unspoken longing he could not easily name. Sweet? If only she knew there was nothing sweet floating through his mind at present.

If anything, it was quite the opposite.

CHAPTER
FIFTEEN

"It is nothing," he countered, not wishing to inflate the matter further than it merited. Yet his gentle reply stirred Rosalind into a state of all sixes and sevens, leaving her even more flustered than she had been in his presence before. His kindness seemed limitless— a cascade of sweet gestures and soft words that, in any lady, would awaken feelings and leave the heart tender. And hers, without doubt, had been touched. She found herself liking the duke far more than she ever imagined she could.

"But it is, Your Grace. I must confess that this evening, when I was forced to wear this gown, I thought my Season was over. Who would wish to dance or be courted when one appears unable to meet one of the *ton's* most adamant rules—that a debutante must radiate the very highest standards of fashion at every event? I failed the moment I stepped into society for the first time. Yet knowing that you have approved my gowns to be made in the colors that truly suit my complexion, I feel that no one has ever done anything so kind for me in all my life."

"Really?" Nathaniel met her eyes, a cynical lift to one of his brows eliciting a laugh from her —a soft, uncertain sound that betrayed her inner conflict.

"Truly. And the other day beneath the willow tree—I will not soon forget that kindness either."

At her words, the duke stiffened, as though the memory of their shared indiscretion weighed heavily upon him. Rosalind longed to know whether that kiss, so unexpected and yet so stirring, had been merely a fleeting mistake or the spark of something she dared to hope might blossom into more.

"Why have you been avoiding me these past days? I thought we were friends," she pressed, studying the shifting emotions that flitted across his face before he once again assumed the composed mask of the duke of Ravensmere.

"I thought it best after our indiscretion—a grave error on my behalf, for which I again apologize and promise never to repeat. I hope you have not been harmed by my actions, Lady Rosalind."

"Lady Rosalind?" she teased, a playful lilt in her tone. "So I am no longer merely Rosalind?"

"We are not in private," he replied coolly,

though his eyes betrayed a lingering conflict as they briefly drifted to her lips.

A mischievous grin lit her features. "Then it is a pity we are not alone, for I would be tempted to see whether that indiscretion was an error or a pleasure we might dare to repeat."

He swallowed hard and glanced away, as if searching for escape in the shadows beyond her shoulder. "We must not repeat our actions. They were foolish and irresponsible—though I bear no blame upon you. I take full responsibility."

A sigh escaped her as she quietly admitted that she had secretly hoped for a chance encounter in a quiet corner of the house—an opportunity to coax him into another stolen moment. She had missed him terribly, nearly driven to distraction by the absence of his daily presence, his voice, the sight of him striding through the halls in all his tall, beautiful majesty. Even his strong backside, seen only in passing, had haunted her thoughts.

"It is not something we should ever repeat. You should not speak in such a manner, and I should chastise you for it," he added, his tone growing severe.

But Rosalind cared little for his reprimand. She believed their initial friendship might yet evolve into something far more meaningful. Was it too foolish to hope? Perhaps she should heed Lady Smithe's advice and focus solely on the Season, rather than pinning her heart on any gentleman who might prove fickle. After all, Lord Felton seemed interested, and she ought to be dancing with him rather than squandering precious moments with her guardian.

"Why ask me to dance if you harbor no interest in me?" she retorted sharply. "I could be dancing with my future husband this very moment, while you ruin it."

The duke—infuriatingly unmuddled—remained calm. "I wished to dance with you, for you are my ward. It would be wrong if I did not share this dance at least once tonight. I needed a moment to explain about your gowns, so that there is no misunderstanding going forward."

Rosalind felt no misunderstanding was needed. The duke had made his position perfectly clear. Yet she could not stifle a flicker of disappointment that perhaps he had once harbored a desire to court her. Since that fateful kiss, she realized in all her three-and-twenty years no other man had ever stirred her as he had.

"Well, you have done so, Your Grace," she replied, her tone edged with both gratitude and resignation. "I think it best that we conclude our dance after this first—there are other gentlemen eager to win my heart and my dowry, and I do not wish to disappoint them."

The duke's lips pursed into a displeased line as his hold on her tightened. In that moment, her body melted against his, every fiber of her being craving his touch, yearning for the feel of his presence. Was she being wanton? When had such desires awakened within her? She had never before acted so impulsively.

"You have not disappointed anyone, Rosalind." His voice was low, strained with conflicting emotions.

"Now, Your Grace—remember, it is Lady Rosalind—we must maintain appearances. You are, after all, my guardian. I would not wish for scandalous rumors to spread about us."

"There is nothing improper about having my ward under my roof with a companion of good repute—a widow of the *ton*, no less. I would challenge anyone who dares cast aspersions upon us."

Rosalind fell into silence, as once again the duke erected a wall between them, a barrier that spoke of regret and a desire to keep the memory of their kiss confined to the past. Perhaps, by kissing him, she had irrevocably altered their friendship. A shame if that was the truth of it.

The dance eventually ended, and he led her back toward where Lady Smithe stood, a handsome gentleman at her side who smiled at Rosalind as she approached.

"Ravensmere, will you do me the honor of introducing me?" The man grinned, his eyes bright with teasing and Rosalind liked him immediately.

The duke nodded, though a tightness marred his expression—an indication that he resented having to perform such a courtesy. Perhaps he longed nothing more than to be rid of her presence until he was forced to attend to her younger sister, Evangeline, the next Season.

"Of course. This is Lady Rosalind, the late Duke Ravensmere's eldest daughter. And this is the Marquess of Issacs," he announced.

"Very nice to meet you, Lady Rosalind," he said, bowing.

Rosalind curtsied in return. "A pleasure, Lord Issacs."

Before she could rise, the marquess clasped her hand and pressed a quick, chaste kiss to her gloved fingers. "The pleasure is all mine." He paused, glancing between her and the duke, who hovered too near for private conversation. "Would you care to dance? A new set is about to begin."

"That would be very kind, my lord. I would like that very much." As she accepted, Rosalind cast a lingering glance at the duke, her chin rising in defiance as she stepped away from him and the ever-present Lady Smithe—a woman who seemed content to remain with the duke for the evening.

Perhaps that was why the duke had avoided

her these past days. He had once claimed a long-standing friendship with Lady Smithe. Were they lovers? Had something secret been unfolding beneath this very roof while Rosalind had been blinded by the intensity of her own feelings?

"This is your first Season, I hear? How are you finding London?" the marquess asked, drawing her into his arms for their first dance.

"Very well. I adore London, and this evening has been the most exhilarating of my life so far. I look forward to many more balls, dinners, and all the delights the Season promises."

"If you would be so kind as to join me on an outing tomorrow—just a short jaunt around Hyde Park, with space in my carriage for your maid—I might make this Season even more entertaining," he offered.

The prospect of visiting Hyde Park with such a handsome admirer thrilled her. "That would be lovely, my lord. I shall ask the duke, though I suspect he will have no objections."

"Indeed. His invitation tonight suggests he believes I would be a suitable match for you."

The marquess's words drew a blush to her cheeks. "I do not know what you mean, my lord," she replied softly.

He laughed—a deep, throaty sound that made her heart flutter. "Oh, but I think you do."

CHAPTER
SIXTEEN

Nathaniel strolled around the ballroom floor, greeting guests and ensuring everyone was enjoying his first ever hosted ball. The evening was meant to celebrate Rosalind's coming out, but it was also a milestone for him, having never held a ball before in his life. So far the night had gone well without any trouble, and everyone appeared to be having a jolly good time.

Rosalind stood out among the revelers. His ward had barely rested between dances before she was whisked away by another handsome, eligible gentleman. Her laughter and radiant smile as she moved about the dance floor was a sight to behold—even if the gown she wore was hideous and suited her not one iota. Yet her smile, her lively manner when she spoke, and the eagerness on the gentlemen's faces as they danced with her only accentuated her natural beauty. Nathaniel caught himself several times halting in his stroll around the room, mesmerized by her beauty and content to simply watch her and revel in her charm.

Damn it all to hell, he needed to get a hold of himself. What kind of man would he be if he seduced his own ward? A woman placed in his care through no fault of her own, only to be taken advantage of by him. Not that she seemed to mind his kisses, but he could not allow that to happen again. If he started kissing her at every chance that presented itself, he would not be able to stop, no matter what society called him when they found out. And eventually society would speak up. There was little that escaped the gossip-hungry matrons of the *ton*.

He rejoined Lady Smithe, who stood alone, and turned to once again watch the dancers on the floor, or at least one in particular. He was doomed for failure.

"Lady Smithe," he said before he could think better of it, "would you care to dance with me?"

Her ladyship beamed at him, and a little apprehension ran down his spine. He hoped Lady Smithe did not read more into his offer than it was—a simple kindness to fill some of the time they had left this evening at the ball.

"How lovely for you to ask, Your Grace," she replied as she placed her hand on his extended one. "I shall like that very much."

He led her out onto the ballroom floor and soon they were dancing, weaving through the crowd and laughing with the other couples enjoying the country-dance.

"How well you dance, Your Grace. You ought to do it more often. I am more than a willing participant. We are friends, are we not?" she remarked.

That blasted term friends would haunt him, he was sure, before the night was out. "We are, my lady, but I fear that if we do partake in too many turns about the room, we shall cause a scandal. No more than two sets is the limit, is it not?" he replied.

She smiled and shrugged. "I do not see the need in only two. We have known each other long enough that no one would suspect anything untoward is going on between us."

She looked at him with an air of wickedness, and his stomach lurched. He appreciated Lady Smithe and all she had done for Rosalind, not to mention that she was the sister-in-law of his closest friend. But more than that, he could not offer anything. Surely she understood he had never seen her in a romantic light. She was a beautiful woman, to be sure, but not the kind who had ever ignited a flame within him.

Before he could speak further, the dance separated them and he reached for his new dance partner only to be paired with Rosalind. He pulled her into his arms, closer than he ought, relishing the feel of her so near after being away from his side most of the night. He could smell the intoxicating scent of jasmine, and he breathed deeply, knowing he would never walk past that climber again without thinking of the woman before him—sweet, and perfect as the white flower that blossomed on it.

Her cheeks were flushed from dancing, and her eyes shone with happiness. "Have you been enjoying yourself?" he asked, though she did not need to answer, it was obvious she had.

"Very much so, Your Grace. This night has been the most exciting of my life. I do not think I shall ever forget it," she replied.

Her most exciting night of her life? What about their kiss? Had that not been the most thrilling adventure she had ever experienced? He shook the thought aside, reminding himself not to be a jealous cur. He ought to be glad she enjoyed her many dance partners, for they might lead to more—even possibly a proposal. The thought of her marrying and leaving filled him with a sour taste, and he tore his gaze away from her, searching for any distraction from the beauty he held in his arms.

"There will be many more nights just like this evening. I promise you as your guardian that it will be so," he said.

She did not respond, and after several heartbeats during which he could not help but glance at her, he did so—a mistake the moment he allowed his eyes to wander. She watched him, her large almond-shaped eyes fixed on his with such intensity that he was certain she could read his mind and uncover all the secrets he fought to hide.

"How delightful, and while we're on the subject of my suitors, Lord Issacs has asked me to accompany him in his carriage tomorrow afternoon. We're to take a ride around Hyde Park at the fashionable hour. My maid will accompany us," she announced.

Nathaniel attempted to speak, his mouth drying at the thought of Rosalind going anywhere with anyone but himself. What the hell was his friend playing at? He knew he could not keep her locked away in this house. She was a debutante, a woman stepping into society for the first time. This was her debut, a ball he hosted so that she may find a match.

He could not now turn around and say she could not go anywhere with a suitor. But his friend? The thought of him whispering sweet nothings in Rosalind's ear made the blood in his veins run cold.

"Are you certain that is such a good idea so soon into your Season? If you are seen about the park with Lord Issacs, other gentlemen may believe your heart is already spoken for and their desire to court you will be halted. I should hate for you to have only one option for a gentleman admirer," he warned.

She frowned before the dance carried her away. He danced with Lady Elliot and then again with Lady Smithe, before once again reaching for Rosalind.

"I do not believe that will be so," she replied as if they had never been separated. "Everyone in society, as I understand it, knows the rules of courtship and that a lady will not promise anything to anyone unless she has received permission from her family or guardian. No one will think that because I took a turn about the park with Lord Issacs, that I have set my cap at him."

"And if he tries to kiss you in the park, forcing your hand into marriage, what then?" Nathaniel wondered aloud. He did not know where that fanciful thought came from, but once it entered his mind, he could not shake it. What if Issacs or anyone tried to force intimacy on Lady Rosalind without her consent?

He ground his teeth, vowing he would call them out and stop anyone who dared to lay even an inch of a finger on her.

"I shall have my maid present, Your Grace. There is no risk."

He growled, pulling her closer than he ought, determined to keep her safe and his alone. The thought propelled him forward until he stumbled before righting himself. "Apologies, Lady Rosalind. My mind is elsewhere," he said.

She raised her brows with an amused smirk on her lips. He frowned, disliking the notion that she might be laughing at him and his possessiveness.

"Clearly, Your Grace." The dance shifted, and he prepared to let her go. "We shall discuss the matter after the ball. I am not certain I can give you leave for such outings."

She moved off into the dance without another word, and he took Lady Smithe by the hand. The conversation was not over, nor could he see himself allowing such an opportunity. If she wished to go about the park, maybe he would be best to do so first. Not some marquess who was not fit to lick her silk slippers. The thought shamed him. Lord Issacs was a good man and friend, and that was the rub of it. He'd invited him to have good company while Rosalind was courted. Nathaniel had not foreseen that he too would throw his hat into the courtship ring.

CHAPTER
SEVENTEEN

I n the early hours of the morning, the last of the guests departed the ducal estate. Nathaniel waved off Lord and Lady Smale, a distinguished couple in their sixties who relished an entertaining ball more than anyone else. Not that he could blame them for overindulging. The evening had been a resounding success.

Rosalind hiccupped at his side before she started up the stairs. Nathaniel turned to watch, giving himself even that little tidbit of pleasure if he could have nothing else. She wobbled and reached for the banister to steady herself and his concern grew. How much had she soused this evening? Was she foxed? He went to her, sensing she may fall and lucky he did so for she stumbled her footing not a moment later. He clasped her about the waist to prevent her from toppling backward and injuring herself.

"Here, let me help you to your room," he said

as he scooped her up into his arms. It might not have been his wisest choice that evening, but once she was safely nestled against his chest, he could not regret the decision.

"Put me down, Your Grace. What will the servants think if they see you?" She giggled as she reached for his jaw, running her fingers over the stubble that had begun to grow. The feel of her touch sent a longing to slice through him that nearly tore him in two. He ground his teeth, unable to pull her hand away from his face.

"You're so handsome." Her thumb brushed over his bottom lip, and he felt an overwhelming urge to bite it, to take her into his mouth and suck on her tender finger.

"Stop," he said through gritted teeth, quickening his pace so they might reach her room faster. "Do not be so familiar. Remember who we both are and where, my lady."

She chuckled, biting her bottom lip and sending heat coursing through his veins. His desire hardened him even further, and damn it to hell, he wanted nothing more than to bite her sweet, plump lip and kiss her into sin.

"I do not wish to remember who I am. Not tonight. Tonight has been a dream." She sighed, and her hand dropped from his face. "I have so many gentlemen admirers I do not know what to do with them all. Perhaps I ought to kiss each of them and see which one suits me best."

Her bedroom door stood slightly ajar. Without thinking, he kicked it open and then, because the thought of her kissing anyone but him sent a red haze of fury to form before his eyes like that of a deranged mythical berserker, he kicked it closed behind him.

"The hell you'll kiss any of them. Not until they have courted you properly and proven themselves worthy of your hand will you ever have the liberty to be alone with them and kiss them," he declared. "Actually no, that will not happen. You shall only kiss one man, whoever has won your heart and will become your husband." What had he been thinking? Certainly he wasn't thinking straight.

He laid Rosalind gently on the bed that her maid had already turned down. She sighed and grinned at him as if she knew a secret he did not. She stretched, placing her hands above her head. The sight of her outstretched on her bed evoked an intimate vision where he could hold her hands hostage, take his fill of her while she cried out his name in longing. Begging him to give her more...

He closed his eyes and forced himself to breathe.

"I think Lord Issacs will be the best kisser of them all. Have you seen his lips, Nathaniel? So plump and juicy. And there is something about his eyes, they seem to shine with wickedness," she murmured with a mischievous laugh as she squirmed on the bed. "Oh yes, I do think he'll be my first and the one I judge all the others against."

Issacs? His friend? The hell she would do anything of the kind. "You will not." Before Nathaniel could think better of it, he found himself on the bed with Rosalind, pinning her arms above her head. His face hovered within a breath of hers. "Over my dead body will you act so rashly with any of the gentlemen who courted you this evening." So close to Rosalind, he could almost taste the champagne on her lips. The scent of jasmine teased his senses, and she smelled so good he could almost eat her.

She stared at him, mockingly. "You cannot stop me, Your Grace. You cannot watch me every second of every ball. And so what if they wish to kiss me?" She pouted, igniting a fire in his soul. "After our kiss, I have discovered that I enjoy the pastime and wish to do it more often than not. Who are you to stop me from having a little fun before I'm married? Are women not allowed to enjoy the same pleasures as men? Are we forever to miss out on what occupies the time of men of your ilk merely because we are female?"

"Yes, damn it, that is exactly what is to occur."

She rolled her eyes, her gaze dropping to his lips. "If I cannot kiss Lord Issacs or any of the other fine specimens of men you presented to me this evening, perhaps you ought to kiss me again so I can have my fill."

"Do not tempt me, Rosalind. You do not know what you ask."

She squirmed beneath him, and with horrifying clarity, he realized he was nearly completely atop her. He could feel the length of her legs, his cock twitched, and he had the sudden urge to press against her like some lovesick swain. Desperate for release.

Not entirely untrue...

"Do I tempt you, Nathaniel?" Her eyes darkened with need and the last tether to his restraint snapped. He released one of her hands and reached down with the other to grasp the hem of her hideous dress.

Meeting her eyes, he did not waver as he slowly slid the material, dragging his hand along the silk of her inner thigh until he reached the apex of her heat. She squirmed, pressing toward his hand before he covered her mons with his palm. A finger stretched down to tease between her folds.

She was wet. Gloriously so.

"Nathaniel..."

His name was a plea, and even though he knew he should stop, he could not change the course of his actions. He wanted her to know pleasure, not from some popinjay lord who could not distinguish one lady from another, but from him, by his own hand.

"Tell me to stop. Tell me that you do not want my touch," he said, offering her an out even as he knew what her answer would be.

"Touch me more."

He ached for her, so damn much. His rock-solid cock strained in his breeches, and he wanted to come. He wanted to spend himself in her, on her, wherever she would allow him.

But he would not. Not tonight, perhaps not ever. Yet he would give her release. That one pleasure he could allow himself—a single night in her arms.

Then he would stop. Stop the madness that raged within him. She was his ward, here to secure a proper and good husband, not some cretin who preyed upon a woman under the safety of his own roof.

Blast, he hated himself, and yet he could not stop.

Her moans of delight and urgent gasps spurred a madness within him that he could not restrain. There was something about being in her arms, giving her what she desired, that he could not deny. He did not want to refute her, even though it was wrong.

He slipped two fingers just inside her heat. Her fingers tightened on his shoulders, her nails scoring his skin.

"Deeper, Nathaniel. Do not tease me," she urged, her eyes heavy with need and burning with expectation. His stomach clenched as he pushed further.

"Mmmm." She licked her lips, closing her eyes in pleasure.

Jesus, he would come in his breeches.

"I want you," she gasped, pressing her body closer. "Stop teasing me so."

Slowly, he obeyed her command, unable to stifle the moan that burst forth. "Fuck you're sweet." He fondled her with his hand, giving her what she craved. He relished the feel of her tight cunny around his fingers, her spread legs inviting him further.

She was a marvel—the sweetest and most sinful woman he had ever known.

Rosalind threw her head back, and he felt the first contractions of her orgasm rip through her. He teased her nub with his thumb as waves of pleasure shattered over her body and danced across her face.

She was utterly breathtaking, stealing his wits and every part of him he had never known could be surrendered.

"Nathaniel, yes..."

He kissed her, needing to taste her on his lips as he wrung out the last of her pleasure.

"Do you like my touch, Rosalind?" he asked, desperate to hear her say it even once.

"Yes, and I want more."

CHAPTER

EIGHTEEN

The following afternoon, Rosalind stood in the foyer, pacing before the large windows that overlooked Grosvenor Square as she waited for Lord Issacs to arrive.

He was late, a surprising turn of events since she had been certain his interest in her had been genuine. Not that it mattered what any of the gentlemen felt for her after last night's ball, as much as she enjoyed the flirtations from other gentlemen, Ravensmere had captured her attention.

What Nathaniel had done to her, however, was an entirely different matter. It was a far more interesting turn of events that she wished to consider. To while away her day in her room and dissect in her mind. Relive every moment. Imagine other scenarios. So many delicious things...

Did he like her more than he wished for her to know?

Was he jealous knowing she was about to go out with another gentleman?

Why had he fled her room so soon after giving her such exquisite pleasure the previous night, as if the devil's Hell Hounds were nipping at his boots?

She had been certain he would join her in her bed, make sweet love to her, ask for her hand in marriage, and sort everything out in her life. She would be married to a man who made her feel so much. Whenever she was around him, her body was not itself. It thrummed and ached, her skin prickled, and even her nipples responded. Another strange turn of events...

She bit her lip and shivered at the thought of the man who occupied her mind—a thought that would plague her far more often than ever before after his actions the previous night. She jumped back from the window as the man himself, the duke, trotted up before the house on his horse and jumped down, handing his mount to a waiting servant. Had he been out this morning? She narrowed her eyes, wondering where he may have gone to.

Just as Nathaniel started up the steps to the front door, a highly polished carriage arrived, and Lord Issacs pulled the brake before jumping down and handing the carriage to another servant.

Wanting to see the interaction, Rosalind

stayed by the window, studying them with interest through the sheer curtains.

Lord Issacs nodded and spoke to the duke, and Nathaniel returned a benign yet confident exchange. They spoke for a minute or two, and as much as Rosalind tried to hear what they were saying, she could not. However, the flexing muscle in Nathaniel's jaw gave her some notion that the duke did not appreciate whatever it was Lord Issacs was saying.

If only she could be bold enough to go outside to join them, to see for herself what they were discussing.

But she had not seen Nathaniel since last night. She had shattered into a million delicious pieces in his arms and now, to face him, to see him again and try to act nonchalant, was a position she wasn't sure she could do.

He made her all sixes and sevens, and yet, in her three-and-twenty years, he was the only man who ever had. Yet he was so accepting of her marrying another, of finding a husband who would suit her. She could not fathom what he was about.

Did he want her for himself or not? She could not wait forever. She was expected to marry this Season, and while marrying one's guardian was not what she had expected or what society would necessarily approve without raised brows, was there anything truly wrong with it? They were so distantly related that even she was not certain how they were family.

But he was determined to remain as he was, and perhaps that was because he had just inherited another title. The man was not without his many duties. She was merely one of them, and perhaps one he needed to rid himself of and as soon as may be, so he could focus on his responsibilities before next year's Season with Lady Evangeline.

Rosalind took a deep, fortifying breath and started for the door, thanking a footman as he opened it. She stepped out into the warm, afternoon sunlight and pasted a smile on her lips, determined not to feel shamed or nervous in front of anyone, especially Nathaniel.

She had done nothing wrong or shameful. Well, maybe a little wrong... But she had experienced what she hoped most women would at some point in their lives. There was nothing criminal with what God had given to fulfill one's desire.

"Your Grace, Lord Issacs, good afternoon," she said, meeting both gentlemen's eyes as she slipped on her gloves, determined to appear as natural and unaffected as possible. Yet within her, her blood pounded loudly in her ears and her skin prickled from being so close to Nathaniel.

Her attention dipped to his hands—fingers that had caressed her most private parts—and she almost bit her lip with longing. She met his eyes, and the heat in his not only warmed her, but they also reduced her to an imaginary pile of ash on the steps.

"Are you ready for our outing, Lady Rosalind? I'm sorry I was late. I was waylaid," said the marquess in his measured tone.

"You were late, Issacs? What kept you?" The duke's tone was reproachful, and Rosalind almost felt pity for the marquess, before a blush stole over his handsome cheeks and he stumbled over his words. She could not help but wonder if he had been engaging in activities similar to hers the previous night.

Taking pity on him, Rosalind moved to his side and slipped her arm about his. "Do not pry, Your Grace. There are many things that could have kept his lordship from our outing, but he is here now, and that is all that matters."

"I heartily agree." Lord Issacs smiled at her, though she could see he had been shamed by the duke and had possibly revealed something the marquess preferred to keep private.

Rosalind's maid stumbled out of the door and was soon assisted to sit on the back of the carriage.

"You're going about Hyde Park, nowhere else mind. I do not want Lady Rosalind's reputation at risk, Issacs. I know you well. Do not forget that we are friends."

"Of course, Your Grace. There is no reason to be concerned. We are chaperoned and merely enjoying a turn about the park. I shall bring Lady Rosalind home so you may keep her under lock and key until the ball this evening," Issacs said, a mocking tilt to his lips.

The Haden ball was scheduled for this evening, and already the modiste had delivered one of her new gowns, much to Lady Smithe's annoyance. The moment her companion had seen the deep-cobalt gown, she had appeared both offended and annoyed simultaneously.

Lord Issacs walked to the carriage, and Rosalind waited at the side so he might help her climb up. Nathaniel's hand wrapped about her upper arm, and he pulled her away from the vehicle, glaring at Lord Issacs as he did so before they were situated a short distance to ensure privacy.

"He's not to touch you. If he does, I'll rip his wandering fingers from his hand. Do you understand, Lady Rosalind?" The deep, rumbling warning from Nathaniel had the opposite effect on her than he expected. His warning only fueled her desires for his grace. She grinned, unable to hide the excitement that thrummed through her veins at his concern, his possessiveness over her.

Perhaps he was more covetous than even he realized.

"Why stop there, Your Grace? Mayhap you

could rip his hands from his arms or his arms from his body," she teased as she stepped close, nearly brushing her breasts against his chest. "If you do not wish for me to be courted by his lordship, you could always ask Lord Issacs to leave and step aside for others. I would not object, but if I am to find a husband, such an order would be seen as odd, to say the least."

She was teasing him, and he knew it well. His nose flared, and the muscle in his jaw flexed. Hell, he was handsome, and the longing that percolated within her was almost too much to bear. She wanted to run her hands through his hair, hold him close as she did last night, clutch him to her as he made her shatter in pleasure.

She wanted everything he could give her, even his very soul.

"Do not sit too close to him. Do not show an eagerness to be in his company. Do not dare touch him, Rosalind."

"I will link my arm with his. Is that allowed? I do not wish to fall from the carriage, Your Grace. I think you're being unreasonable."

In that sense he was, but still, she adored that he was warning her away from the marquess. How delightful it was for a man to be jealous without even realizing that was exactly what he was doing.

He pursed his lips, and the scowl between his brows deepened. "Hold on to the carriage. There is no need for you to touch his person. Do you understand?"

"But if his lordship continues to court me and asks for my hand, I shall do a lot more than link my arm with his. I shall have to allow him to touch me wherever it pleases him then."

His face turned thunderous, and for a moment Rosalind thought she had gone too far.

In fact, perhaps she had.

CHAPTER

NINETEEN

At Rosalind's words, Nathaniel saw red. Instead of ripping Lord Issacs from his perch atop his carriage and tearing his arms from his person to stop him from ever touching Rosalind, he simply stepped back. He attempted to gain some semblance of control, although that was far from possible at that moment. What on earth was wrong with him these days? Every waking hour was filled with images and thoughts of Rosalind. He lived for the moments when he caught a glimpse of her in the house—reading a book quietly in the drawing room, playing the piano, or heading out on one of her many shopping expeditions with Lady Smithe.

He was obsessed, and his preoccupation needed to end. Here and now.

She turned and started for the carriage, and it was not long before she was perched against Issacs, her arms safely linked with his. He bit back a sharp retort that sat on the end of his tongue and instead waved them off, forcing a serene smile onto his lips as he did so. Not that he believed Rosalind thought he was happy she was gallivanting about London with a rogue who had once been as busy in the boudoirs of London as he had been before inheriting the dukedom. Nathaniel knew this better than anyone, since Issacs was one of his closest friends.

He stormed inside and sat at his desk, staring out the window for several minutes as he thought, planned, and chastised himself for the fool he was being. He told himself he was not interested in his ward. The lie taunted him for the falsehood it was. He was interested in Rosalind and, damn it all to hell, she seemed to be enjoying his company and the time they spent alone together.

He shifted in his chair until he caught sight of a missive on his desk. He picked it up, broke the seal, and scanned it quickly. Before he had finished reading the note, he was striding through the house, then yard, heading for the mews. It took only minutes for his stable hand to saddle a horse, and soon he was on his way to Cheapside. The ride through Mayfair and into the surrounding area was thankfully brief and without incident.

Nathaniel stared up at the modest yet clean

and tidy dwelling. The houses here resembled those in Mayfair but on a much smaller scale. Far more people lived in this community than his own, many engaged in trade or law. He rapped on the door and heard people in the house. He waited patiently, but when the door opened, Nathaniel felt the blood drain from his face. A young woman opened the door, and he stared, unable to comprehend how similar in looks and coloring she was to Lady Rosalind. They could be sisters... He chastised himself for the fool he was. They were sisters, half by blood.

Nathaniel rallied his resolve and attempted to school his features. "Good afternoon, I'm the Duke of Ravensmere. I was hoping I could come in so we can discuss the missive you sent..." He offered a small smile. "If you're willing?"

The young woman opened the door wider and stepped aside. He moved past her and she closed the door, locking it before retreating deeper into the house. Nathaniel followed. Two other young ladies, younger than the one who had opened the door, sat on the stairs watching him. Both were too similar in appearance to the Ravensmere daughters back in Hampshire. The duke's blood obviously ran deep in his daughter's veins.

He followed the elder sister into a small sitting room where a modest fire burned. She sat, placed her hands in her lap, and gestured for him to do the same. He complied and looked around, noting a few expensive pieces of furniture that might have come from the ducal London townhouse before they lost everything they had ever known.

"So, Your Grace, you are the new duke. How fortunate you are to inherit a most worthy title."

He narrowed his eyes and nodded, unwilling to share that the late duke had left barely enough funds to keep the London house running, let alone his country estate. A worthy title it may once have been, but not under the late duke's watch.

"Thank you." He met her eyes and was again startled by how much she reminded him of Rosalind. "I'm sorry to speak so bluntly, but I understand you're the late duke's illegitimate family and you wished an audience with me."

"We are," she said as she raised her chin, her defiance uncanny to Rosalind's. Nathaniel sighed inwardly. Even here in Cheapside he could not stop thinking of his ward—a woman who, at that moment, was enjoying another man's company. The slight was unbearable.

"I'm Miss Helena, but there is no need to apologize for your words, Your Grace. Do not great men such as yourself always speak with a blunt tongue?"

He did not respond, but he knew all too well how true that statement was. "Is your mother here? Perhaps I could speak to her regarding the situation in which we now find ourselves."

The young woman's face paled as she shook her head. "Our mother passed only a few days after our father. A broken heart, the doctor said."

Nathaniel had not known that, and it shamed him. "I'm sorry for your loss."

"Thank you, but it was some time ago now and we're trying our best to manage."

Again Nathaniel looked about the room. "And that brings me to your missive..."

The young woman glanced at her hands, wringing them together in her lap. Nathaniel could tell she had not wanted to reach out to ask anything of him, but with two younger sisters to care for, when one was desperate, one was willing to do anything, he supposed.

"Yes, the letter." She adjusted her seat and gathered herself. "I'm desperate, Your Grace. I've taken in laundry to try to bring in some income to help with food, but I've had to let go of our one maid, and soon I shall have to let go of our cook as well. We are barely surviving, and I'm fraught with fear for me and my siblings."

"Did the duke leave you with any financial compensation?" he asked, already knowing the answer, for it would be the same as what the late duke had left his legitimate children.

"No, only this house, which I'm thankful cannot be taken away from us. I do not wish to bring in any boarders, not with my sisters here. One can never quite trust anyone in London, and well..." She bit her lip as tears welled in her eyes. "Please help us. With Mama gone, the stipend my father left us ceased with her passing. An oversight I'm sure His Grace had not thought of."

Nathaniel sighed and glanced out into the foyer where the two younger sisters remained on the stairs, watching him through the banister.

"Of course I shall be of assistance, but if I am to help you until you are all married and settled, you must refrain from letting it be known who your father is and the connection you have with his daughters. I am their guardian now, and I am attempting to have each of them married over the coming years. I do not wish the scandal of the duke having a second family to injure their chances."

The young woman looked at him, her features brimming with hope for the first time that day. "Oh, of course, Your Grace. We have always been a secret of sorts, and we understand. We do not wish to be known as illegitimate or bastards in society either. We could not bear such shame that was not of our making."

"Very well then, it is settled. I shall bestow a sizable living on your household and a small dowry for each of you should you wish to marry. It will not be much, but it will help you find matches that are more becoming than perhaps those you might have married otherwise."

"You're too kind, thank you, Your Grace. I do not know what to say." Miss Helena fumbled for her handkerchief and dabbed at her cheeks and nose. "I've been so terribly worried and not knowing what to do." She paused. "Shamefully, I had a gentleman at the markets just last Sunday ask my price, and for a shocking moment I panicked at the thought of what I might become."

"No, I shall not allow that. You are the late Duke Ravensmere's daughters, legitimate or not. You do not deserve such disgrace. I shall do right by you, even if your father did not."

"Please do not be too harsh on Papa. He was a kind and loving father, even if he was unable to care for us once he passed."

Nathaniel stood, and so did Miss Helena. "I will have to disagree with you on that point I'm afraid. Your father, while kind to you and your mama, was not the same with his legitimate daughters. They may have the titles and grand homes, but you had the love of a father that they never received and are far poorer for it."

Miss Helena nodded and escorted him to the door. "Thank you again for coming. I know you were not obligated to, but I thought it best to ask you to come here instead of the Mayfair home."

"You are right. The late duke's daughters do not know you exist. His Grace never told them, and I think it would be a shock and hurt them dearly to learn he had another family entirely. I do hope you'll keep your promise and remain secret, for both you and the Ravensmere family."

"Of course, Your Grace. We promise to be discreet."

Just as he preferred. "Thank you."

CHAPTER
TWENTY

Rosalind sat in the carriage and held on to Lord Issacs as they made their way around the park. The day was clear with a blue sky and not a breath of wind. The park was full to the brim with people taking the air, having picnics, or, like herself, enjoying an outing with a gentleman admirer.

Lord Issacs spoke of many things. The conversation was not at all stilted, although most of the topics pertained to himself, his horses, and his estates. She was almost thankful when he turned the carriage for home, and they headed back toward Grosvenor Square.

The man was a kind gentleman, but unfortunately she did not feel an ounce of excitement when around him. The only time it was amusing was when the duke was nearby and she could tease His Grace that she was on an outing with another man and not himself.

"I do hope we can ride again, Lady Rosalind. I found your company most pleasing, and I hope you did in return."

"That would be most pleasant, my lord." Although right at this moment Rosalind could not think what else they would speak about. The weather perhaps, or the state of the roads leading into London from Hampshire? "I shall wait eagerly to receive my invitation for another ride about the park," she said, remaining polite.

"Very good."

Once home, his lordship jumped down before turning to help her alight. Even when she took his hand there was no jolt of awareness, no longing that tore through her and Rosalind could definitely state that his lordship was not for her.

"Good afternoon, my lord," Rosalind said, waving him off as she stood at the door with her maid before heading inside. "I do not think I can bear going out again with Lord Issacs. If I hear any more about him or his horses, I believe I shall know him better than he does."

Her maid laughed and covered her mouth with her hand. "He did indeed speak much on the subject, but perhaps he was merely nervous."

"He could have been, but I did not think the outing would ever end. I do not think I like him any more than a friend."

"Lady Rosalind." The duke's commanding voice startled her and made her jump. Her maid started up the stairs toward her room, leaving them alone in the foyer.

"How did the outing go with Issacs? I hope he was on his best behavior?" the duke asked, watching her keenly.

"He was," she replied, hoping that the boredom creeping into her tone was not noticeable. She cleared her throat and attempted to sound more enthusiastic. "He's very nice and such a gentleman. He wishes to escort me on another outing soon."

"Well, that is good news."

She attempted not to frown but knew she had failed. "I did not think you would find such information pleasing, Your Grace. I did not think you wished me within a foot of the man."

"Well, that was the guardian coming out in me, and nothing else. I do not want to see you ruined before you can make a great match."

Rosalind wanted to stomp her foot. What was it with the duke who ran hot and cold? Why could he not run hot all of the time? He was much more malleable when warm.

"You've said that before, but do not worry, Your Grace." She moved closer to him, ensuring privacy. "I will not allow Lord Issacs the liberties I've allowed you. My reputation in that regard is safe."

She smirked and turned to leave, but before she could move toward the stairs, he clasped her hand and dragged her into the dining room. He slammed the door and pushed her hard against it.

Rosalind gasped, yet her body came alive, burned, and ached almost the moment he touched her. She clasped the lapels of his coat and relished the sight of his wild, uncontrolled gaze that slammed into her and made her feel everything she had ever wished for.

The man teetered on the brink of losing control, and she wanted to push him over that precipice to see what would happen next. His fingers spiked into her hair, lifting her gaze to meet his. He dipped his head so that his lips were but a breath from hers. She could almost taste his sweet lips. She had been dreaming of kissing him again since the moment he left her room, which now seemed like eons ago—far too long between such delectable interludes.

"I cannot think straight when I'm around you," he murmured.

She ran her hand down the lapels of his coat and slipped them around his waist. His body was warm under his jacket, and she could feel the tension as he fought what he desired and what he believed to be honorable. Yet there was nothing dishonorable about desiring a woman, especially her. She wanted so very much for him to kiss her.

Would he already and cease this longing that ripped her in two?

"Then do not think at all, Nathaniel." She pressed herself against him, even though he held her firmly against the wall. Her lower body undulated against his, seeking the release he had given her a taste of the other evening.

Her actions seemed to snap his control, and his body responded, hardening against hers. His hand slipped around her bottom, cupping her cheek, his fingers flexing against her flesh before he wrenched her close.

Rosalind gasped. She could feel everything—his hardness pressed against her like a rod. Truly wanton, Rosalind hooked her leg around his hip and assisted him teasing where they both ached and sought release.

"Damn you, Rosalind." His lips brushed hers, and she sought more of his kiss before he pulled back. He ground his manhood against her sensitive, weeping cunny, and she moaned, her fingers clawing into his back. "The things I want to do to you. If only you knew, you would flee back to Hampshire."

"Or I may not," she whispered, undulating against him, her body not her own, so focused on gaining release and feeling the exquisite sensations of coming apart in his arms. She needed to feel that again. She was desperate for it.

He lifted her fully in his arms, his manhood pressed at her core as he slid against her undergarments and teased her, moving her toward release.

"I need to hear you call my name. I'm going to make you come so hard that you'll never look at another man the same," he declared.

Rosalind was already of that mind, regardless of what they were doing at that moment. She could not imagine undertaking such a thing with anyone else other than Nathaniel. Yet, did he understand what he was saying in the throes of passion? She doubted it, or perhaps he would regret it soon after. But she could be patient, and in time he too might see that they were perfect for each other. They certainly sparked whenever they were near to each other, and that in itself was not always so certain between people.

He rubbed her cunny, teasing her. Moisture pooled between her legs, and she held on, desperate for him and everything he could give her. His manhood seemed to grow larger, and she longed desperately to touch him, to tease him and learn every secret about his person.

But there was no time for that now—not here, at least—but perhaps another time when she could corner him in a private location in the house where they would not be interrupted.

"Nathaniel." The moan tore from her as exquisite sensations trembled through her core and throughout her body. Nathaniel kissed her hard, catching her cry with his lips.

"Rosalind..."

He worked against her, his movements frantic but never quite enough. She held on to him, wringing from his person every ounce of her release, wanting to savor the moment forever. His eyes met hers, heavy with desire and satisfaction. She clasped his jaw, desperate to capture his image in her mind so she could forever remember this moment.

"I do not know what I'm doing with you," he confessed.

Rosalind understood his words and his concerns. He was her guardian—a man destined to see her married to another this Season—and yet, right now, knowing everything about the man in her arms, the man who made her feel so wonderfully alive, he was the only one she had ever wanted.

"We are not doing anything wrong, Nathaniel. We are distantly related, and although you are my guardian, we are of a similar age. I do not care what society thinks, and I do not want your fear of their judgments to ruin what is clearly happening between us," she declared.

"And what is that exactly?" He helped her back onto her feet, and Rosalind adjusted her gown, ensuring everything was as it should be.

"Well, I do not know about you, but I like you

very much. I know it is bold of me to say, but I have enjoyed our friendship, and I certainly relish how you make me feel. I want you to make me feel that way more often." She stepped close, brushed her lips against his, and felt tension ripple through him. "Don't be scared of me, Nathaniel. I won't bite. I promise."

He closed his eyes, a pained expression flittering across his handsome face. "Christ, Rosalind." He opened his eyes and held hers. "You're driving me to distraction."

She grinned, savoring that she had managed to provoke him. She longed to drive him to the point where he might agree to be one of her gentlemen admirers and, perhaps, even ask for her hand in marriage.

Nathaniel as her future husband would do very well.

TWENTY-ONE

T he following evening was the Lygon ball, one of the larger events in London each Season and a ball to which anyone who was anyone wanted to attend. Nathaniel's attendance—even before he had become the Duke Ravensmere—had been secured by his friendship with Lord Lygon who hosted with his dear mama ever since the death of his father several years before.

Nathaniel had not escorted Rosalind and Lady Smithe to the ball, even though as Rosalind's guardian he ought to have. Shamefully, he had remained at Whites most of the day, preferring to eat his meals there too, before returning home, bathing, and changing for the ball—well after the time Rosalind and Lady Smithe were to depart for the event. He greeted his hosts, shaking hands with Lord Lygon and bussing the cheek of the dowager Viscountess Lygon before making his way into the room.

The ballroom was full to the brim. Hundreds of guests danced and gossiped both in the ballroom itself and in the few antechambers the family had opened for the evening. From here, Nathaniel could see that the terrace doors were open, and people milled outdoors, taking the air and a break from the revelries inside.

A group of boisterous and eager gentlemen stood huddled near the side of the room. Their laughter and animated appearance caught his attention. Nathaniel watched them for several heartbeats before a cold shiver ran down his spine at the sight of who had caught their approval and notice.

Rosalind.

She stood before them all like a reigning queen ready to be obeyed, and each of the young bucks was eager to do her bidding. As he drank in the sight of her, his mouth gaped at the vision she formed—utterly breathtaking. This evening she wore a royal-blue empire gown with delicate, puffy sleeves that sat on her slim, pretty shoulders. Shoulders he'd kissed and wanted to do so again. Her hair was swept up in curls atop her head, accented by a blue ribbon tied throughout her dark locks. Her lips smiled, her cheeks pinkened, and Nathaniel knew she was enjoying the gentlemen's company.

No doubt every one of them was giving her compliments. And why should they not? She was a beautiful woman, kind, generous, and passionate. So damn passionate he had spent in his breeches yesterday in the dining room of all places. Not that he could regret their interlude. Even now his cock twitched at the memory. Fuck. He needed to stop thinking of her in that way, and certainly not at social events. No one wanted to see him walking around with his cock leading the way.

Her words had haunted him, and it was one of the reasons he had been a coward and remained at Whites the entire day. He should not let society concern him regarding their guardian-ward position. But if they got wind that something romantic was happening between them while she lived under his roof, her reputation would be ruined. Not to mention her sisters by association. And with Rosalind unaware that she also had half sisters in London—sisters who were children of a mistress and illegitimate—should that scandal break, there would be no telling what damage it could do for the women he was tasked with looking after. He could not, should not, add to the troubles that could befall her and them both should any of that information come to light.

Still, Nathaniel found himself situated not far from where Rosalind stood, being courted by an array of young bucks, with Issacs there too, standing beside her and crowing to anyone who would listen that he had already had an outing with Lady Rosalind. He sipped his whisky and tried not to appear surly and disgruntled not only at his friend, but the others also. But inside he was seething.

He hated every moment of her being surrounded by other men. She was so utterly breathtaking this evening that it was no surprise the men flocked to her. Lady Smithe, whom he could see standing not far from Rosalind, looked as put out as he was—but for entirely different reasons, he presumed. The woman was a widow, rich and still attractive, but she was not Rosalind. There was a hardness to Lady Smithe that Rosalind did not possess, and he assumed it had something to do with Lady Smithe being too opinionated and cutting when she did not think someone warranted her time.

Rosalind, however, was the type of person who would stop and talk to anyone and help them if she could. She was too noble—far too good for him. He had never been the type of gentleman to do anything that did not benefit him. Giving the Ravensmere daughters a dowry each was proof of that. Selfishly, he wanted to be rid of them as soon as they hit the marriage mart, not because he had a kind heart. Paying the illegitimate daughters of the late duke to remain quiet served his purpose too, though it was beneficial to both. The duke's second family did not want to live as paupers or lose their home, for such a life would be hard for women of their ilk. But after meeting Rosalind, he wanted to do better, be better—and yet in that he had failed miserably.

At every opportunity, he dragged her into a room and touched her, drank from her lips, fondled innocent flesh he had no right to touch. He was not her husband. He should be keeping his hands to himself. And still he did not. He was a bastard.

Lady Smithe spotted him and sauntered over, turning to watch Rosalind as she was escorted out onto the dance floor.

"Lady Rosalind is quite the entertainment this evening. I do hope she's not leading the gentlemen on more than she ought. I may have to speak to her regarding her approach to the opposite sex. She's been quite forward at times..."

Lady Smithe's tone held a little too much venom for Nathaniel's liking, and he glanced at her, noting her pinched mouth and narrowed eyes. "How are you getting on as Lady Rosalind's companion? I had hoped you were friends, but I fear I may be mistaken by what you say."

Her eyes widened and she schooled her features, the opposite of what they had been a moment before. Nathaniel was not convinced, no matter what she said next.

"Oh no, she's the dearest girl—I just worry for her so. Living in the country for so many years has put her at a disadvantage, and I fear the *ton* may eat her alive if we're not vigilant."

That at least was true, if he did not eat Rosalind first. The thought shamed him, and he frowned as he watched Rosalind laugh at something Lord Kelter said on the dance floor. Her attention flitted about the room before she locked eyes with him. A small, knowing smile lifted her lips and heat churned in his gut. He swallowed the need that rose within him. The woman was a minx and knew exactly what she was doing when she looked at him that way— as if every thought of what they had done yesterday afternoon in the dining room fluttered through her mind. Just as it had been on repeat in his own head, torturing him, taunting him, making him want to leave his room when he had gone to bed last evening and stride up to her door to see how many liberties she allowed him when they were alone. He feared he knew too well, and the thought almost buckled his knees. Dear God, whatever would he do?

"Perhaps you could make your presence known more in the circle of admirers, so they might be more willing to conform to expectations and not become too boisterous or eager."

"I shall do what you suggest. Now," Lady Smithe said, slipping her arm around his, "will you ask an old friend to dance? I fear that widowhood has caused me to become a matron no one asks to dance."

Nathaniel inwardly sighed. He had no plans to dance this evening, at least not with anyone other than Rosalind. Still, Lady Smithe was an old friend—even if she could be prickly at times. He took pity on her and led her onto the floor, pulling her into his arms and into the dance with ease.

For several turns around the room, he did not speak, nor did he take much notice of the happenings around him, lost in his thoughts. But the scent of jasmine raised his awareness, and he looked up to see Rosalind watching him from the arms of her dance partner, her face carefully schooled so much so that he could not discern her thoughts. Still, he could not look away, wishing he were the one holding Rosalind in his arms, not that popinjay Kelter.

He was a doomed man indeed, and there was little hope for him coming out of the Season alive.

TWENTY-TWO

Rosalind could assure herself, without any uncertain terms, that she did not like seeing Nathaniel dancing with anyone —most especially not with her companion, Lady Smithe. The woman, she was certain, did not like her. In fact, Rosalind was sure that Lady Smithe tolerated her at best and not very well at that. Yet seeing Nathaniel dancing and witnessing Lady Smithe's conceited smile whenever someone watched them made Rosalind's covetousness rise.

Did Lady Smithe want Nathaniel in the same way that Rosalind did? She could not blame her if that were the case. But if her ladyship intended to claim Nathaniel for herself, she would do so at her own peril. Rosalind was not the type of woman to give up on something she wanted without a fight, and she wanted Nathaniel. Desperately.

The dance came to an end, and Rosalind watched with morbid fascination as Nathaniel lifted Lady Smithe's hand and kissed the back of her glove. His laughter and smile made envy simmer hot in her veins. What was he about, being so familiar with her ladyship after all they had done together?

"Let me escort you back to your companion, Lady Rosalind," Lord Kelter said, pulling her from her interest.

"Thank you, my lord," she replied, regaining her composure as she returned to her many admirers who stood nearby Lady Smithe and the duke. Rosalind schooled her features, hoping her face did not betray the turmoil raging within her.

Was the duke trying to make her jealous? Was he attempting to convince himself that they could not be together and that he ought to be with another—Lady Smithe perchance? The thought made him a fool if he believed, even for a minute, that such a union would work. Lady Smithe, while undoubtedly lusting after the duke, would soon grow disillusioned with him when he did not fall at her feet with every whim. Her annoyance would grow, and then so would her derision and dislike. No, they would never work. But the duke and Rosalind—well, that was something she needed to convince him of before he gave Lady Smithe more hope than was fair.

"You dance most beautifully, Lady Rosalind.

One would never believe that you have lived so long in the country without society," the earl remarked offhandedly.

She fought not to state that although from the country, she was far from uneducated or non-accomplished. "Thank you, my lord, that is very kind. But my sisters and I often practiced, so we are well versed in the current dances in town," she replied.

"I do not doubt it." Lord Kelter grinned mischievously and, just as the duke had with Lady Smithe, picked up her hand and kissed the back of her glove.

Rosalind smiled, but there were no butterflies, no hope or desire that coursed through her —merely a pleasant exchange between two people destined to remain friends. Lord Kelter deposited her back with her admirers, along with Nathaniel and Lady Smithe.

His lordship strode off with a spring in his step and the duke cleared his throat. His scowl toward the departing viscount clear to anyone who might be watching.

"You look very happy, Lady Rosalind," Lady Smithe observed, her face beaming after her dance with the duke and his evident pleasure in it.

"I am, my lady. Lord Kelter is a very nice man, and I would dance with him again if he asked."

"You are only permitted one dance per gentleman per night. There will be no raised brows when it comes to *my* ward." The way the duke accentuated the word *my* caught Rosalind's attention, and she raised her brow, uncertain—after his eager dance with Lady Smithe—that he should refer to anyone as his property.

"You can have no objections to Lady Rosalind dancing with Lord Kelter again. She is allowed two dances per evening." Lady Smithe studied the duke for a moment, and Rosalind wondered if she was curious about his dislike of the gentlemen courting her. "You do wish your ward to marry, do you not?"

Nathaniel fumbled to find his words before managing to reply, "Of course, Lady Smithe. I am merely concerned for her reputation."

Rosalind scoffed and bit her lip as she realized she had mocked the duke's words. In truth, he was being rather absurd and overprotective—especially when he could not hold her in his arms at this very moment and claim her as his, nor would he. He had no right to be overbearing when it came to the men he was so determined should marry her.

"Lady Rosalind, remember the rules of courtship. A gentleman may dance with you twice, but no more. You must never be alone and unchaperoned at any time. You must not use our given names when speaking to one another. A lady listens more than she speaks."

Rosalind met Nathaniel's gaze as Lady Smithe recited some of the rules, leaving many others unsaid. Already, she had been using the duke's given name, and they had been alone together in both the carriage and the house. The memory of what had transpired in the dining room the previous day haunted her, and she longed for the same intimacy again—even if he was being unagreeable and surly this evening.

"I understand perfectly and shall keep everything you said in mind," she replied.

Lady Smithe smiled and, spotting another acquaintance, left Rosalind alone with Nathaniel.

Rosalind stepped close to him, ensuring their conversation remained private. "Whatever shall Lady Smithe say if she knew we were using our given names in private? I'm certain she would suffer an apoplexy if she heard what else we have done."

"Are you threatening me?" Nathaniel's cold tone startled her, and her gaze flew to his, expecting a response to her jest but finding him staring with cold, hard eyes devoid of mirth.

"No, of course not. Why would you say such a thing or think it?" His words sent a chill through her, and all enjoyment for the night vanished at his disapproval. She had never been vindictive, and now pain wedged in her chest that he would think her so. He said nothing more, merely turned his attention to the dancers before them, remaining quiet and aloof.

Rosalind placed space between them, debating her next move. Part of her wanted to rail at him for daring to be so rude. How could he touch her and kiss her as he had, only to chastise her as if she were a child incapable of distinguishing right from wrong? She knew what they were doing was wrong—they were unmarried, and she was his ward. She was a maid, and he was a rake. But she was not a silly child to be spoken to so disrespectfully, especially when he was so eager to engage in all those wicked acts a gentleman ought not to do when unsupervised.

"I'm waiting for an apology, Your Grace. Whenever you're ready," she said, watching him, hoping he would feel a twinge of unease.

A muscle worked in his jaw, yet stubbornly he offered no apology. "You should take a turn about the room and dance with other gentlemen before the night is over. You are wasting your time here with me."

Perhaps that was true. Was she wasting her time and hopes by pinning them on the wrong man—one who clearly cared more for society's opinion far more than his own heart? A man does not touch a woman and speak such sweet words without having his own heart stirred. He was a fool, but she would not allow herself to be duped into falling into his arms only to be treated like the muck under his boots when they were in public.

"Yes, well, perhaps I should take a turn. There are other gentlemen present this evening who are far more agreeable than you." She paused and glanced over her shoulder. "You may leave. Lady Smithe will see me home safely when the ball is over. There is no need for my guardian to lord it over everyone and scare them away. Goodnight, Your Grace."

Rosalind turned up her nose and went in search of her admirers and the few female friends she had made during her coming-out ball. Her eyes stung, and she swallowed hard. She would not cry over a man. How dare she be so emotional simply because he was the first to make her feel anything beyond boredom?

She needed to give other gentlemen the opportunity to gain her interest—surely there would be more than one man on this fabulous green earth to make her heart race and her stomach flutter. It was statistically impossible for the duke to be the only one.

Impossible.

CHAPTER

TWENTY-THREE

Rosalind sat in the carriage, quiet and contemplative as they made their way home from the Lygon ball. That she was not speaking to him, Nathaniel could understand, and he hated himself for having to put up a wall to try to save her from whatever it was they were doing. What he was doing—seeking her out, pulling her into rooms, and kissing her to within an inch of her life—was entirely his fault.

He watched her, unable to keep his gaze from her profile as she observed the streets of Mayfair slipping by. Hell, she was beautiful—a woman who made him feel completely discombobulated just by being in her presence. Not that he would tell her such a thing. She already held too much power over him. He did not need her to know any more than that.

"Did you have a pleasant evening?" he asked,

knowing that she appeared to have, while he had watched on in agony, forced to listen to Lady Smithe slip between concerned chaperone and scathing gossipmonger. Not that she was performing her duty this evening—no, she had stayed at the ball and was nowhere to be found when it was time for them to leave. So they had departed without her ladyship. No doubt tomorrow that too would be another matter for which he would be admonished.

"Very pleasant, thank you. I believe the tea we're hosting this afternoon shall be full to the brim with interested gentlemen."

Nathaniel glanced out the window as the dawn kissed the stone buildings of London. "I hope they're all suitable," he stated, knowing full well that he could not control every facet of her life, no matter how much he wished to.

She looked at him then, her eyes void of warmth. "More suitable than you, Your Grace. None of them pulled me into the dining room and pawed me like you did, if that is what you're asking."

He swallowed the bile rising in his throat, hating that she was angry with him. "I'm sorry for my conduct. You deserve so much more than what I gave you. I'm ashamed of how I treated you."

She shook her head, her mouth pursing into a displeased line. "You... you are asha— How dare you kiss me, want me as you do, and then become frigid, colder than the Scottish Highlands? I do not believe what you're saying. I do not believe that you do not care for me or want me still, so stop pretending to have a moral compass when you do not possess one."

He fisted his hands at his sides before clutching them to stop himself from sitting beside her. To explain himself clearly, nothing else. "But I should have refrained from kissing you or touching you as I did. It was wrong and reprehensible."

She growled and punched her seat. "Stop it, Nathaniel. Stop pretending that what we did was wrong. I've never felt anything so right before in my life. I come alive in your arms, and you damn well know it, so stop saying I'm a regret—that you do not want me—because I know that you do. I know that you burn as much as I burn for you too."

"But it is wicked, and I need to mend what I did or I'll never forgive myself. I cannot have you ruined. To do so puts your siblings at risk, and that is not fair to any of them. I feel like an old man who is salivating after a woman I am supposed to look out for. Men such as those I've ridiculed in the past—and here I am, doing the same."

"You are only three years my senior, not some ancient relic old enough to be my grandfather."

"I will not touch you again. You must look elsewhere for your husband, as you have done so this evening. Passion between people does not mean that we would suit as husband and wife, and I shall not have either of our names sullied by more gossip. I am responsible for you. That is where this relationship must end."

She stared at him, clearly flummoxed by his words that ran contrary to his actions these past weeks. He turned to look out the window—anywhere but at Rosalind. He hated seeing the disappointment in her eyes, yet he believed that in time she would be thankful that he allowed her to find a true and unwavering love somewhere else.

"Very well, Your Grace, whatever you wish, but know this. I shall never allow you to touch me, kiss me, or try to have any intimate relations with me again from this night forward. Do not come to me regretting your choice, for I will not hear of it. I do not like to be played the fool, and that you've made me do so is unforgivable. I will not allow it a second time."

Her words struck ice through his veins, and he swallowed the bile rising in his throat, knowing she meant every word. That he would never touch her again—to feel the softness yet eagerness of her mouth—left him bereft. As hard as his choice had been, it was for the best. He was certain of it, and in time she would be grateful for his restraint.

The carriage rolled to a halt, and before a footman could run to open the door, Rosalind had pushed it open and was hastily making her way indoors.

Nathaniel watched her leave. A war raged within him—wanting to call her back and then wanting her to go. Guardians did not marry their wards. The idea was both proper and vile, and many would forever raise their brows in disgust should it come to pass.

She disappeared into the house, and he climbed down to follow her. Instead of retiring to his rooms, he walked into his study. No matter the many appointments the day would bring, he was not quite ready for bed just yet. He would lie there and think, stare at the ceiling, and debate his choices—whether they were good or bad. Right now, everything felt wrong. So, so wrong.

L ater that same day, the afternoon tea was a success by all accounts, but Nathaniel could think of nothing worse than watching a parade of young bucks—or at least men of his acquaintance, some of them friends—lining up to court Rosalind. He sipped his tea, hoping the beverage would wake him from the nightmare of his own making. This was what he wanted Rosalind to do, and judging by the cloying men surrounding her and listening to her every word, that was exactly what she was doing. She had not looked at him once, nor had she even bid him a good afternoon when she entered the room with Lady Smithe, who too seemed to be engrossed in her afternoon gossip with several friends of her age.

Nathaniel swallowed a sigh and leaned back in his chair, welcoming the sight of Lord Issacs as he entered the room. Instead of heading directly to Rosalind, the marquess came and sat beside him.

"Ravensmere, how are you this afternoon? You look tired, my friend. Is the excitement of the Season keeping you up at night?" he asked.

The mischievous glint in his friend's eyes put Nathaniel on guard, and he wondered if there was talk already about him being a guardian to a woman who was only three years his junior. Or was the man merely niggling him since they were friends and Issacs had taken a liking to his charge?

"Not at all. What gives you that impression?" Nathaniel replied.

"Well, look, my friend," Issacs said, gesturing toward Rosalind. "Being the guardian to a young woman of means and beauty must be a massive undertaking for a man used to doing whatever he wishes whenever he pleases. It is not for the faint of heart."

"Do not tell me you're serious in your pursuit to win her heart? I know all there is to know about you, Issacs, and I do believe I'd find you lacking the requirements to be a husband if you were serious and not merely making sport of me having to play guardian." Not that Lord Issacs wasn't handsome or wealthy—but he was a rake through and through, preferring the chase to the catch. He was not for Rosalind.

"I have not yet made up my mind. She is indeed a beauty, but I am not certain I want a wife this year. Flirting is fun. That is all I have come here for this afternoon. I must keep you on your toes, Ravensmere—a little taste of your own medicine and all that."

"What a good friend you are." Nathaniel shook his head, glad that at least Issacs was not pursuing Rosalind seriously. His attention turned back to Rosalind, and he froze the moment he witnessed a small, folded note being handed to her from Lord Felton.

The fiend.

How dare he act so recklessly and fast! He would need to have a word with Rosalind about that note and find out what was in it so he could shove it down Felton's throat. Something he would do when he had the bastard alone, where no one could see what he'd do to him when he did.

CHAPTER
TWENTY-FOUR

After the afternoon tea, Rosalind's curiosity got the better of her as she strolled into the gardens to read what Lord Felton had written. She opened the missive and scanned its contents quickly:

My lady fair, grant me but one sweet chance,
To claim your hand for love, not just for a dance.
No whispered gossip, nor the ton's decree,
Shall ever keep my heart from thee.

Heat bloomed on her cheeks as she stared at the words. Did Lord Felton truly feel that way about her? She certainly enjoyed the company of the gentleman. He was amusing and made her laugh a great deal, yet she had never considered him a poet or a romantic. Her body did not incline toward romanticizing him in the least, although perhaps he did have a hidden side that longed for love and a happy marriage.

Maybe she would be a fool to push him aside in the hopes that Nathaniel would change his mind, come to his senses, and see that the harmony burning between them was real and tangible—something he should not ignore lest he lose it forever. Despite having warned him that she would never let him touch her again, Rosalind knew the words were a lie the moment she uttered them. Of course she would let him touch her again. She still wanted him, even if his actions left her frustrated and annoyed. All he needed to do was to touch her and she would crumble into a ball of wants and needs.

"Lady Rosalind," sounded a voice near the terrace.

Rosalind turned to see Lady Smithe walking toward her with a small, determined smile on her face—a marked change from the usual disappointment she wore when they spoke. Rosalind was certain that the woman was not her friend. In fact, she sometimes wondered why she had agreed to be her companion at all.

Rosalind stopped walking and slipped the note back into her pocket, but before she could ask how her ladyship's day was progressing, Lady Smithe reached into her pocket without a by-your-leave and stole the note. She waved it accusingly in front of Rosalind's nose. Rosalind attempted to snatch it back but Lady Smithe was too quick and she was unable to.

"Give that back," Rosalind demanded, reaching for it.

But her ladyship was too quick and she opened the note, reading it quickly before looking at Rosalind with disgust. "I did not want to believe it, but the duke was right. Do you know how scandalous it is to accept a secretive note from an admiring gentleman? You cannot accept such gifts."

Rosalind stilled at her words as anger thrummed through her veins. Nathaniel had told Lady Smithe. Was he a snitch now too? "It is nothing, my lady. Please do not make more of the situation than it warrants," she said, bored with the conversation already.

"The duke certainly thinks it warrants me knowing of it." Lady Smithe shook her head, contemplating her next words. "Really, child...what are you thinking acting so fast?"

"I'm not a child. We're the same age, Lady Smithe. Do not be so disrespectful and remember your place. You are my companion, not my mama or guardian. Do not overstep your bounds." Rosalind did not mean to snap at her ladyship, but really, did the woman not see the absurdness of her chastisement?

"How dare you talk to me in such a way!"

Lady Smithe's eyes welled with tears. "And after all the kindness I have afforded you!"

Had she afforded Rosalind much kindness? Rosalind could only recall a handful of occasions, and those had only been when the duke or someone of value—in her ladyship's opinion—was present. Still, it was not in Rosalind's nature to be cutting or cross, and she took pity on Lady Smithe.

"I do not wish to quarrel, my lady. I do appreciate all that you are doing for me, but I did not send a note in return to Lord Felton. There is little chance this exchange between us will end in scandal."

"There were several gossiping matrons of the *ton* at the afternoon tea. Any one of them could have seen and is right now shadowing as many drawing rooms as they can, to speak of what they saw. I would not be surprised if at tonight's ball you are the talk of London."

The horror of such a thought stilled Rosalind's heart, but she rallied herself, unwilling to believe that anything of the sort would occur. She had done nothing wrong.

"All will be well, my lady," she whispered, wishing her tone sounded more confident than it did.

"All will be well, shall it, child?"

Rosalind bit back a retort at Lady Smithe's repeated use of the term child. Clearly, the woman wanted to prickle under Rosalind's skin.

Lady Smithe lifted the note and read it again, her lips pursing into a puckered frown. "The man clearly wishes to have a rendezvous with you. This letter is practically vulgar." She paused. "The duke must read it posthaste."

"Do not show the duke, I beg you," Rosalind pleaded, reaching for the note again, but Lady Smithe was too quick. She started back toward the house, her determined steps too eager to stem from real concern, and not the outcome she wished to realise. That of Rosalind being chastised like a silly girl and made to look the fool.

Rosalind followed quickly without running like a lunatic. Lady Smithe, hasty on her feet, stumbled into the duke's office without knocking, and Rosalind followed. The duke looked up from the many ledgers spread out before him, a frown between his handsome brows as he took in the two of them.

Lady Smithe, the snake that the woman was turning into, strolled toward the duke's desk as if she were holding some precious ancient artifact instead of a scribbled verse from a gentleman caller.

"Your Grace, indeed, you were right. Lady Rosalind has fallen from grace and is communicating with Lord Felton. Look at this missive—it is quite telling that there is something between the two. I think it may be wise to invite the gentleman over and discuss his intentions."

Rosalind rolled her eyes, having never heard of anything so preposterous. "Oh, do be serious, Lady Smithe. I have not been communicating with him at all."

"Then explain what the duke saw and what I am holding right now in my hand."

"You're holding a note he handed to me that I did not respond to. That is all."

The duke took the outstretched note from Lady Smithe, read it, then screwed it up and threw it toward the fireplace.

"Are you in communication with Lord Felton?" Nathaniel asked.

His question hurt more than Rosalind wished to admit, and she met his gaze, determined not to be made out as some wanton she was not—at least not around the earl. As for the man sitting before her, watching her every nuance, that was another matter altogether.

"Only when we speak at afternoon teas and balls, just like everyone else."

"I do not believe her, Your Grace. You must check her before it is too late and she is ruined, along with her sisters."

"You're not to be alone with Lord Felton going forward, and certainly communication of this kind must end. Do you understand?" His tone sounded more cold and distant then ever she'd heard it before.

Rosalind gaped. Who was this man before her? She did not recognize the emotionless, disapproving gentleman who had once swept her up into his warmth and brought her to life. "I have not been alone with him and do not appreciate the notion that I have been."

A muscle worked in Nathaniel's jaw, and he glanced at Lady Smithe, who looked on between them with an amused, self-satisfied smirk that twisted her normally pretty visage into something ugly and conniving. Rosalind would no longer be fooled into believing that the lady had any inclination or desire to be her friend.

"His lordship certainly thinks that whatever has been happening between you is proof enough of your feelings for him and his willingness to send you love notes."

Rosalind shook her head. "I will not listen to this any longer." She started for the door, but did not get far before the commanding, hard voice of the duke stopped her in her tracks.

"You have not been dismissed."

Rosalind turned and glared at the duke, disgusted by how he had treated her over something so irrelevant. Before he could say another word, she turned on her heel, ripped the door open, and stormed through it. She ignored the sound of Lady Smithe's shocked gasp and the resounding wails.

"Oh, I'm so terribly sorry, Your Grace. I have let you down with our charge."

How absurd was that woman, and how infuriating was the duke! Rosalind stormed up the stairs, and just as she reached her room, a hand reached out and clasped her arm, spinning her about. She looked up at the duke, ignoring the spark of desire that ignited within her at his touch. She was angry with him, and she would not bow to his absurd accusations. She would not.

Damn it all to hell. She wouldn't.

CHAPTER
TWENTY-FIVE

"Are you in love with Lord Felton?" His question burst forth before he could think of anything else to say. He had so many things he wished to express to the woman in his arms—the very woman whom he longed for and dreamed about every hour of every day. The mere thought of her with the earl had almost made his head explode, and reading the missive had nearly stripped him of all self-control, so that he might bellow at the world—and Rosalind, too.

Damn it all to hell, he needed to get a grip on himself and his emotions.

"And what if I am? Is that not what you want me to be?" She raised her chin, and he longed to clasp it, tilt it upward, and kiss her into submission.

Her answer, however, threw his mind into turmoil, and he could not think straight nor form the words to agree with her. He should, of course. That was why Rosalind was in London—to find a husband and marry.

The sound of footsteps on the stairs interrupted them, and he stepped away, letting go of her arm and schooling his features. He could not go after her in such a manner.

She was right, of course. He was blowing hot and cold, and he needed to stop. He had told her to marry someone else, to fall in love, and he needed to let her do so.

"So long as you keep your reputation intact, that is what I wish. But in the future, do not pass notes with anyone. It is not becoming of a lady of your stature, and can raise eyebrows if the knowledge becomes public."

Rosalind's eyes narrowed, and Nathaniel had never seen her look at him with such loathing. Yet that was exactly what he wanted her to feel for him. Any other way would have led them to end up in each other's arms until they lost their senses entirely.

"You're a hypocrite. Stay away from me." Rosalind turned on her heel, walked into her room and slammed the door in his face. He sighed and closed his eyes, hating that she now detested him. He despised that he had been unable to control his emotions, wants, and needs around her, and now she was hurt and upset, angry with him.

"Come, Your Grace." Lady Smithe linked her arm with his. Unable to rally any denial, he allowed her to lead him back downstairs to his office. "I shall speak to Rosalind when she has calmed down and all will be well. She's a dear girl, and I'm certain that Lord Felton's courtship is honest and above board. We are just not used to being in positions of responsibility, and we too must bend and learn throughout the Season."

All true, he could not argue her points. Still, as he sat behind his desk with work strewn out before him, he could think of nothing else except the woman upstairs who was seething over his actions. He hated himself for hurting her.

"I'll be attending the Tatton ball this evening, Lady Smithe, so I shall help you chaperone Lady Rosalind. We shall ensure that Lord Felton is genuine before we allow him any more leave with our charge." If he allowed him within an inch of Rosalind at all.

"Very good, Your Grace. Until tonight."

Lady Smithe left him then, alone thankfully, so that he could sit and think. Dwell in his own misery. That was more the truth of it.

Later that evening at the Tatton ball, Nathaniel once again was forced to watch his ward be escorted about the room, danced with until her smile was as wide as ever and her cheeks pink with pleasure.

Knowing she was angry and upset, he was relieved to see her enjoying her time in London. He took comfort in the fact that her admirers were many and that she was never without friends or good company. A bittersweet emotion washed over him as he downed the last of his whisky and called over a footman for another glass. This was how it was supposed to be. This was him fulfilling his duty.

Lord Kelter escorted Lady Rosalind to his side, and disappointment stabbed at Nathaniel that she did not give him any attention or greeting. She merely stood beside him, animatedly speaking with Lord Kelter and giving him the cut direct.

Nothing that he didn't deserve.

"I say," Lord Kelter said with a smile, "how lovely it is to have the Ravensmere family back in London. The legitimate ones, at least."

His lordship laughed and Nathaniel almost spat out his whisky at the viscount's words. He stilled and looked to Rosalind who frowned at his lordship as if he'd sprouted a second head.

"Excuse me, my lord? Legitimate? Whatever do you mean?"

"Oh, well, as to that," Lord Kelter stuttered, catching Nathaniel's eye before clutching at his cravat as if it were too tight. And it would be a noose about the bastard's throat if he did not keep his mouth closed. Nathaniel glared at him, warning him not to say a word, and Lord Kelter stumbled over his reply, unsure and weary as his gaze darted between Nathaniel and Rosalind.

"Nothing, my lady. I misspoke."

Rosalind, quick of mind and tongue, did not seem swayed. "No, you did not misspeak, my lord. But I am interested in knowing what you meant by *legitimate Ravensmeres*. Are there illegitimate ones?" She laughed, but when Lord Kelter did not, silence soon fell between them.

"Your Grace?" she asked, meeting Nathaniel's eyes directly. A question in hers that he did not wish to answer.

Dear lord, what would he say? What could he say? He had hoped she would never come to know what her father was about in London while they were huddled away in the country like orphans.

"Would you care to dance?" he asked, trying to change the subject and avoid answering her query.

She crossed her arms and shook her head. "No, I do not wish to, but you, Lord Kelter, will answer me and tell me what you meant by those words if the duke will not."

"I ah... Well...it is not confirmed. No one really knows for sure..."

Nathaniel cleared his throat. Was it hot in

this ballroom? Why was the space so stuffy? "Come, let us dance, Lady Rosalind. I have not had the pleasure this evening."

"And nor will you," she replied curtly. "Now tell me, Lord Kelter," she demanded, her voice brooking no argument.

The viscount sighed, and Nathaniel winced, knowing the fellow was about to crumble.

"There is a rumor, Lady Rosalind. Possibly the worst-kept secret in all of London, but your late father, the duke, had a mistress. With his association with that woman, he fathered three daughters. Illegitimate Ravensmeres. That is all I meant." Lord Kelter looked down at his boots, shamed by his own big mouth. "If you'll excuse me. I think I see someone...Lord and Lady...is after me."

Rosalind rounded on Nathaniel, and he steeled himself for the coming conversation.

"My father fathered children in London, and you did not tell me?" she demanded as she pushed past him. He followed close on her heels, trying to keep up as she slipped through the crowd, her determination to leave after such news obvious to all who noted her distress. He caught up to her just as she hailed a hackney cab, forgoing the ducal carriage.

"How long have you known this?" she demanded, her body all but radiating with tension.

He stood at her side and ran a hand through

his hair, wishing he had told her and that she had not found out by some slip of the tongue from some foolish fop. "I've known since I inherited the title."

She looked up at him, her eyes welling with tears. "So everyone in London knows that my father had a family here in town—illegitimate ones—while his legitimate children rotted away in the country."

The carriage rolled to a halt before them, and he went to assist her up, but she pushed his hand aside, calling out a direction and attempting to close the door on him before he could join her.

He ignored her wish to be alone and climbed in, sitting across from her. "Not everyone knows, but people suspect, yes. The duke allowed them to live at the London home on Grosvenor Square. That is probably why he never sent for you girls to come to town."

She gaped, and he hated the duke in that moment for hurting her—for crushing and possibly squeezing the last ounce of love she held for her father from her soul.

"My room—it was decorated so nicely. That wasn't for us at all, was it? The room used to be another's." She paused, looking out the window as she wiped a tear from her cheek. "Whose room was it?"

Nathaniel rubbed the bridge of his nose as an ache began to thump between his eyes. "The room was Miss Helena's room prior to them being forced to leave the moment the duke passed."

"And where are they now?" she asked, watching him from the shadows. He could see she was upset. He longed to go to her, to comfort her, but he dared not. She was not in that state of mind—and perhaps might never be again, not with him.

"Cheapside. The duke purchased them a home prior to his death to ensure they would not be homeless."

She nodded. "So he loved them?" There was bitterness and hurt in her tone and he could not blame her for it.

The pain in her voice tore him in two, but he could not lie. "Yes, he loved them very much."

Just as he feared that he loved Rosalind more than anything or anyone in the world, even himself. He hated seeing her in pain. He wanted her happiness and contentment, nothing else would do. He sighed, unsure what to say or do to make any of what she learned right. "I'm sorry, Rosalind. I should have told you."

She looked out the window, quiet and contemplative. "Yes, someone should have."

TWENTY-SIX

Rosalind could not believe what information Lord Kelter had bestowed on her this evening, nor that Nathaniel had kept such an important secret from her. Yet why that surprised her, she did not know. They were not friends anymore. In fact, he was beginning to resemble a man she did not recognize at all.

She paced her bedroom and rang for her maid, wanting to exchange her ballgown for something much more comfortable. Her maid arrived only minutes later—a welcome distraction from the relentless churn of her thoughts.

"Good evening, my lady. You called?" The maid dipped into a curtsy, before hanging two gowns into her armoire.

"Can you help me undress, please? This evening's events are completed, and I wish to retire early tonight," Rosalind stated, her mind a whirl of who her stepsisters were and what they were like. Were they kind, or sharp tongued like Lady Smithe? Would they care to know who their family was? Was that even a possibility for them all, knowing they were illegitimate? What were the rules? Rosalind did not know when it came to such matters.

"Of course, my lady." Mary began to unclip her gown, slipping it down her body and, for the first time this evening, Rosalind felt as though she could breathe. She quickly untied her stays, tossing it onto a nearby chair.

"Is everything well, Lady Rosalind?" the maid inquired gently. "You are very quiet this evening."

"I'm perfectly well, Mary, thank you," Rosalind lied, sitting on the edge of her bed to remove her stockings. "Why wouldn't I be?"

"Well..." The maid hesitated before coming over to take Rosalind's silk stockings and placing her slippers by her feet. "Lady Smithe returned from the ball an hour or so ago, and she was in quite a state. She went into the duke's library, and I have not seen her since. I thought that something may have gone astray."

Something certainly had gone astray. Did Lady Smithe's return and countenance mean that the *ton* knew her father's secret for certain now? She stared at the unlit hearth, before dread and something ugly and fearful crawled up Rosalind's spine that had nothing to do with her half sisters. She stood abruptly and went to her armoire and pulled out her pelisse, tying it quickly at her front.

"All is well, Mary. You may head to bed yourself if you like. I will not be needing you again this evening."

Her maid smiled, pleased by the early dismissal. "Very good, my lady. I wish you a good night and shall see you in the morning."

"Goodnight, Mary."

Rosalind waited several minutes after her maid had left before she exited her room and headed downstairs. If the duke and Lady Smithe were talking about her illegitimate sisters, then that was a conversation she needed to be part of. Moreover, the fact that Lady Smithe had returned from the ball troubled suggested that perhaps the *ton* knew of her family's disgrace—thanks to Lord Kelter blurting such information out so publicly and with so many ears listening. Would that hurt her chances of making a good match?

She did not wish to think of any other possibilities as to why the duke and her companion were nestled in the library alone at this late hour. The thought did not bear thinking, and yet, she frowned, her stomach lurching at the horrible thought in conjured.

Determined to find out the truth, no matter

what the situation was downstairs, Rosalind left her room and headed down to see what the duke and Lady Smithe were discussing before she retired for the night. There were no staff about at this late hour—the footman who guarded the front door nowhere to be seen.

Rosalind heard the muffled voices first—the duke and Lady Smithe speaking—but she could not make out their words. She approached the library door that was slightly ajar and listened. She shouldn't of course, it was bad form and extremely rude, but the sound of Lady Smithe's words rooted her to the spot. It was not the usual forthright and confident tone of her ladyship. Oh no, it was a seductive, soft, cajoling tenor she'd never heard before.

Her stomach knotted, and she pushed the door open needing to see the truth of the situation for herself. Her possible ruination in the eyes of the *ton* due to Lord Kelter's admission thrown from her mind.

Standing before the hearth were the duke and Lady Smithe—Lady Smithe's hands resting on the lapels of His Grace's coat, his hands fastened about her waist. Rosalind gaped, and a small squeal of alarm escaped her lips before she could stop it.

The duke was a rogue. She understood that most men of his ilk were, however after everything they had done together—the soft whispers in the night, the passionate kisses that had stolen her wits and her heart—she had believed it meant something. Clearly, from the sight before her, it meant nothing at all.

"Rosalind," the duke called as he moved toward her, all but throwing Lady Smithe to the side.

Rosalind raised her hand, halting his steps. "My apologies, Your Grace. I did not know... That is to say..." she faltered, unable to find the words to describe what she had witnessed. The lump in her throat hurt to speak through and she swallowed several times before she managed to get out her next words. "I'm sorry for interrupting you, excuse me if you will."

"No, wait, Rosalind." The duke's footsteps rang loud in her ears, but she did not wait to see if he was indeed following her. Instead, she ran through the foyer, blindly out into the drawing room and onto the terrace and gardens beyond. She needed air—lovely, fresh, cooling air where she could think and possibly cry if her blurred vision were anything to go by.

Could this night become any worse than it was already?

She ran until she stood on the lawns, her slippers ruined by the grass, and looked up at the starlit sky. His Grace's aversion to her over the past week made more sense now than it had an hour ago. He was courting Lady Smithe. Of course he was, and she had been a fool to think that a woman of her limited sensual knowledge would garner the interest of such a virile, handsome man. Although he wasn't so kind if he could taunt her as he did and then move on to another woman without a by-your-leave.

The fiend.

She swallowed the lump in her throat and took a deep breath, anything to calm the panic that tumbled in her stomach. Her chest hurt and for a moment she thought she may faint.

"Rosalind, wait." He strode toward her purposefully across the yard and she hated that even now he appeared like a vision of everything she wanted in a husband. A strong, capable man who made her want things. Want everything.

She raised her chin, determined to be strong and not cry in front of him. She could do that later in her room. What she wasn't prepared to note was the fear and regret tumbling about in his green gaze. The man was a fool if he thought she would believe anything he said to try to explain away what she saw.

"Wait for what, Your Grace?" she stated matter-of-factly, glad her voice did not wobble. "Wait for you to push me away again—to not even treat me as your friend, so you are free to do as you please with Lady Smithe?" She gestured toward the house, ignoring how the vision of the duke blurred with her unshed tears. "You need to leave and return indoors. There is nothing for you here. Not anymore."

"No, no, you have it all wrong. I'm not courting Lady Smithe. I have never seen her in a romantic light. She was upset about the rumor of your father's illegitimate family. It is now the latest scandal in London, and I'm sorry for that, but she cornered me in the study—she was crying. I comforted her, and at some point during that exchange, she thought there might be more between us. There is not. I have assured her of that, and she has retired for the night."

"I do not believe you." Rosalind pushed past him, and in two quick steps he was behind her, hauling her back to face him.

"Stop, damn it, and listen to me. I was not doing anything with Lady Smithe. I promise you."

"You lie—that is all I know. You lied about us being friends. We are not. Not anymore. You lied about my father having another family and keeping me in the dark. The *ton* may openly know now, though others must have suspected before tonight's ball, and I wonder how many laughed at me when my back was turned. And as for Lady Smithe—I know what I saw. Are you trying to say that I did not see you embracing? That you were not clutching her waist?"

Rosalind swallowed the bile that rose in her throat at the thought of what might have happened between them if she had not interrupted. The idea of Nathaniel being intimate with anyone sent dread through her every fiber, leaving her uncertain of what to do with herself. He confounded her, and she was not herself when she was around him. Did not know how to be strong and protect her heart.

"I did not tell you about your stepfamily because I did not want you to be hurt by your father any more than you already were. Miss Helena assured me she would not cause trouble for you, and I thought the matter was settled."

"Miss Helena?" she asked, her mind racing as to what else the duke had done behind her back. "You've spoken to my father's illegitimate daughters?"

The duke ran a hand through his hair, staring at her as if he did not know up from down. "Rosalind, I'm sorry, but I did speak to them. They have no income, no assets other than the house —nothing to keep it warm during winter, or to feed them most days. The younger two are but fourteen and so I offered them funds in return for their discretion and to keep them out of your way."

"You bribed them?" Though it pleased her that they would not be left destitute, Rosalind was appalled that Nathaniel had persuaded them to remain silent—a dirty little secret her father had kept for years and now the new duke wanting the same. How she loathed powerful men right at that moment.

"I did not see it that way, and I hope Miss Helena does not either. My intentions were only to keep you and your reputation safe. To ensure a suitable match for your hand."

"Yes," she spat, venom in her tone. "So I may marry some gentleman—a man who says all the right things to me during the many balls and parties we attend, who then proposes, luring me into a false sense of security, while all the while I do not know if he is sincere. Not really. I shall find out that truth when we marry. When I'm in his marriage bed and behind his grand walls, yes?"

She started for the house once more and managed to get inside the drawing room before Nathaniel stopped her yet again.

"Do not be angry with me, please," the duke pleaded. "It is only you that I thought of."

She pushed his hand off her arm, stepping away from him. "That is little comfort right now. I need to go to my room to think—and hopefully to sleep."

"Rosalind, please. Know that I do not want Lady Smithe..."

Rosalind turned and left the room. Frustratingly a small part of her hoped he would confess to wanting her instead, that he'd made a mistake and did not wish to lose her, but he did not. Despair swamped her and she made her room before the tears began to fall unheeded. If tonight had proven anything, it was that there was no future here. Not with the Duke of Ravensmere. Perhaps not even within the *ton*.

TWENTY-SEVEN

B y the following evening the news of the late duke's inability to keep his mistress and their offspring a secret became the hottest tidbit of gossip around London. And a week after the scandal had broken, Lady Smithe, although only too willing to try to kiss Nathaniel in his library, now avoided him at every ball and dinner they attended. A cynical part of him couldn't help but wonder if her ladyship would ask to leave soon, not wish to be tainted by association to a family that could not behave. Save her reputation from being corrupted by mere proximity.

Rosalind stood beside him at the St. George ball, as beautiful and untouchable as ever, but this evening society's idea of what a diamond of the first water should be had shifted—and Rosalind was no longer it. Although several men had danced with her, including the blasted buffle-headed Lord Kelter, many had neither returned to her side nor engaged her in conversation.

"I fear your hope that I shall marry this Season will come to nothing now, Your Grace. I'm being given the cut obtuse, it would seem. How quickly the *ton* turns. I had heard it was so, but I did not think it would be so hasty," Rosalind declared, her tone sharp.

Her words cut him to his core and he hated she had been found wanting by people who had no right to judge. Rosalind had done nothing wrong and was an innocent party in all the mess her father had left. The *ton* ought to be ashamed of themselves.

An intense urge to punish Lord Kelter for opening his bloody mouth overwhelmed him. Not that she didn't deserve to know the truth—of course she did—but he never wished for Rosalind to be injured as she now was. Not that he could save her from the hurt such news would bring. Rosalind was destined to be wounded no matter when or how she found out about her family.

"If you do not receive an offer of marriage, then the men are all fools." Nathaniel included himself in that statement—not that he believed Rosalind wished to hear such things from him. Not anymore.

She had barely spoken a word to him the past week. Whenever she looked at him, he had an inkling of what being loathed felt like. He had ruined everything between them, and he did not know how to restore their friendship. He inwardly cursed at the thought.

To hell with friendship—he wanted her, all of her, including her heart. The past week, being apart from her, feeling the distance growing between them had put paid to his determination to keep her away. He could not do it. Nor did he want to. To hell with the society who turned their back on a wonderful woman. They could all go hang.

"I do not wish to remain. I want to leave," she declared, her voice quavering in distress.

He nodded and waved for Lady Smithe to join them. That her ladyship, seeing his gesture, promptly turned her back and ignored his command sent fire through his blood. The audacity! He would dismiss her and hire a new companion posthaste. Nathaniel held out his arm, and Rosalind took it before he escorted her out of the ball.

"Lady Rosalind, Your Grace, I was just coming to find you," Lord Felton called as he walked toward them.

Inwardly, Nathaniel groaned at the sight of the earl. He wanted to be gone, away from this glittering society whose honor was only as deep as the material of one's gown. His lordship bowed before Rosalind, smiling mischievously.

Although Rosalind had not enjoyed the evening so far, it pleased Nathaniel to see one of her beaus bowing before her and happy to be in her presence.

"I've come to ask for a dance, my lady. There is a lively set coming up next, which I think will be enjoyable, if you're willing," he declared.

Rosalind bit her lip, and the image that conjured in Nathaniel's mind was everything it should not have been. He glanced at Lord Felton, whose attention was fixed on Rosalind's mouth also, and it took all Nathaniel's willpower not to throttle the rogue right then and there in the ballroom.

"I suppose one more dance will not hurt, if we can delay our leaving, Your Grace?"

"Of course," he said, stepping aside. Nathaniel watched as Rosalind was escorted away, feeling utterly bereft now that she was no longer by his side. He was a lovesick fool who needed to act before it was too late—before men such as Lord Felton, who clearly did not care about the idle gossip, made it their mission to claim Rosalind forever.

R osalind was thankful for the dance with Lord Felton. For the first set, his company had been excellent—amusing and distracting from the worries that plagued her. What she had come to rely on whenever they were together. However, during the second, he watched her so intently that it left her uneasy, and she did not know if there was something amiss.

"My dearest Lady Rosalind, how are you faring this evening? Now that we're mostly alone, I wanted to mention that during the past week I have heard the terrible things that involve your family and could hardly believe any of it was true," his lordship said, his tone mocking, his face one of fabricated pity.

She inwardly groaned, not wanting to discuss her father. The late duke had caused so much strife for her and her sisters that, even in death, he remained a burden. "The gossip is not of my doing, and I know little of the particulars," she lied. "I do not think we should discuss the matter, my lord." Hoping that would put an end to the conversation, Rosalind threw herself into the dance, and for several steps his lordship remained silent, but her reprieve was short-lived.

"I'm sorry that the *ton* have been so hard on you, even though you are not responsible for your father's actions. But to have had those bastards living in your home—I should think the new duke ought to have them booted from London so they may never injure a woman as pure and beautiful as you."

His words, even if well intended, stirred an annoyance in her. She despised the word bastard when it referred to children unable to choose how and when they came into the world. She possibly loathed the word as much as she hated gossipmongers who did not know when to stop a conversation, even when told.

"My half siblings, for that is what they are, my lord, are innocent in this situation just as I am. I hold no ill will toward them," she said.

"You do not?" The earl raised his brow. "They are children of a courtesan. I am certain you do not share such morals, unless—"

"Unless what, my lord?" Rosalind interrupted as she stepped from Lord Felton's arms, daring him to say what she feared. How dare he be so rude and cruel, especially when they had been friends up until tonight?

"Well, if you sympathize with the likes and kinds of people that are the illegitimate children of the duke, mayhap you're not the jewel everyone believed you to be," he spat, snarling like a rabid dog.

Who was this man?

Before she could think to respond, or react, a fist connected with the earl's nose, snapping his lordship's head back. The sight was not one that Rosalind thought ever to view with joy, but, after his lordship's cruel words, she did.

Lord Felton toppled backward, squealing as he did so before landing hard on his bottom. He clasped his nose, his eyes welling with tears from the force of the assault. "How dare you, Your Grace? I should call you out," Felton gasped.

"How dare I? How dare you speak to Lady Rosalind in such a way. Be thankful that I do not bloody more of your body or call you out as well. You are not fit enough to lick her slippers, let alone court her," Nathaniel retorted.

"I would not court her for anything now."

"Good, for I would not want you too," Nathaniel snapped. "You are not worthy of her hand."

Stunned, Rosalind said nothing as Nathaniel took her hand and dragged her from the room. The ball—once a hive of activity—fell deathly quiet as they summoned the carriage.

"I'm sorry Felton dared speak to you in such a way. I will make your Season right, Rosalind. I will not have you ruined by all this gossip," Nathaniel declared.

Rosalind watched him, unable to believe that he had defended her honor so publicly. The duke wrenched the carriage door open as it pulled up before them, and she noted that his knuckles were a little red and one was cut.

She climbed into the carriage and sat, waiting for him to join her. It was not long before the vehicle lurched forward, and they were on their way home.

"You're hurt?" she asked, moving to sit beside him and taking his hand to inspect it.

"It seems Lord Felton has a bony nose," he said. "But I think he's worse for wear than I am," the duke replied, a small smile lifting his lips.

She bit her lip to stifle a chuckle at the madness that had befallen everyone. "Thank you for defending my honor. He was out of line and quite vicious. I did not think people could be so false, but I was wrong."

"The *ton* is full of vipers. One must always be on guard." His fingers linked with hers, and a little of her annoyance toward him for keeping secrets—and for pulling away from whatever was happening between them—dissipated. As for her fears of Lady Smithe clawing her way into the duke's heart, she had but kept her distance from them both this week, and something told Rosalind her ladyship's aversion to the duke was because of his shunning of her kiss and nothing else.

"I do not like it when we're not together, when we're not friends," he murmured, playing with her fingers, keeping her hand in his lap.

"Is that what we are, Your Grace? Friends?" she asked softly.

"Is there another term for it?" he inquired.

She met his eyes and saw the question burning in his dark gaze. "I hoped we were becoming lovers." There, she had said it—what she longed for most. Still longed for no matter how mad she had been at him. The man was a fool, but she hoped he would become her fool.

He closed his eyes for a moment, a pained expression crossing his handsome features. "I'm your guardian. It's wrong of me, and yet..." He reached for her, clasped her face in his hands and met her gaze. "I want you to be mine, Rosalind."

"You do?" she asked, uncertainty shading her voice. "Do you mean only here and now, or forever?" She needed clarity, perfect transparency before she could give him her answer.

Rosalind did not hear his reply to her question before he took her lips in a searing kiss, erasing all thought entirely. But then, it was blissful being in his arms so she could forgive him his lapse in concentration.

CHAPTER
TWENTY-EIGHT

Nathaniel could no longer remain aloof, cold, and distant from Rosalind. As surely as one cannot breathe underwater, he could not endure another day apart from her side. He adored her. Though they had scarcely known one another, she had become his home—the other half of his soul.

"I'm sorry, Rosalind. Please, say you'll forgive me for being such a cad," he pleaded.

Her fingers tightened around the lapels of his coat as he struggled to quell the burning need within—a need he doubted would ever be quenched, even if she were to consent to be his forever.

"You do not want this," she murmured, attempting to pull away, but he drew her closer, unwilling to let her slip from his grasp.

"I do. I do want this," he insisted, his voice earnest. "I was troubled—not solely by what society might say about a guardian marrying his ward, for I am new to the dukedom—but by your father's notorious reputation. We have learned all too well of the life he once led in town, a life spoken of only in hushed tones. I feared that his name would forever be linked with recklessness and disregard for our strict customs. I did not wish you or your sisters to suffer further, and in my misguided caution, I pushed you away whenever we grew close. I will not," he declared, pressing his forehead against hers. "I will never do so again."

Her eyes searched his, seeking the truth in his gaze. And he was sincere—never had he been more certain of anything in his life. The callousness of Lord Felton had been the catalyst, and he could not abide any slight against her. She was far too good to suffer mistreatment.

He loved her...

"I need to know," she said, drawing back just enough to create a space he both abhorred and tolerated. "Did you kiss Lady Smithe? Has something been transpiring between you during my time in London?"

"No. Not at all." He clasped her hands, squeezing them as he cursed the chill of her silk gloves. "She did try—I admit it—and I rebuked her advance, for which she has been surly ever since. But I swear upon my life that I have touched no other woman since I met you. There is only you."

"Truly?" A small smile played upon her lips, and he exhaled a sigh of relief. Perhaps he could yet regain her trust—and, if fortune favored him, her love.

"Truly. I dream and breathe nothing but you, Rosalind. These past days apart have rendered me nearly useless. I cannot concentrate, and my bookwork piles up while the sight of you dancing and enjoying your events—though I rejoice in your happiness—is a kind of torment to me." He paused, gathering his resolve before adding, "I've fallen in love with you."

Her eyes widened before filling with tears. He drew her into his arms, holding her close as she nestled against him.

"From the moment you stormed into your house in Hampshire, I was utterly partial to you. You captivated me from our very first conversation, and I believe there is no one else in the world as loving and kindhearted as you. For that tender heart, I beg your forgiveness for my recent foolishness. Allow me to make amends for the rest of our lives—as husband and wife."

Rosalind stared at Nathaniel, scarcely able to fathom how a night could transform from disaster into utter bliss. He loved her? He wished to marry her? She pulled back, gathering her wits so as not to act rashly. Yet the fear she read in his eyes—that he might be denied, that she might say no—dissolved the last vestiges of her anger.

Although she abhorred secrets, she could understand his reluctance to mention her illegitimate sisters or to divulge that Lady Smithe had attempted to kiss him. And while it did not surprise her that any woman might be drawn to a man like Nathaniel, she believed his rebuff was his way of protecting her honor.

"I will marry you, Nathaniel, for I love you too —so very much," she declared, relief pouring through her that she had been brave enough to say it.

He smiled and laughed, gently shaking her shoulders. "You do not jest?" he exclaimed, then pressed a quick kiss to her lips. "Tell me you speak in earnest, for I could not bear it if you did not."

"I mean every word," she replied with a soft chuckle, reaching for him.

He claimed her lips in a kiss that stole her breath and swept away all thoughts of their surroundings and uncertain future. In that moment, every worry vanished.

She pushed him back onto the settee and straddled his lap, yearning to be close—to kiss him and feel the warmth of his touch. He did not disappoint. Clasping her tightly, his fingers glided along the back of her gown, sending shivers cascading over her skin.

"I want you so much," he murmured.

"And I you," she answered, her voice husky with desire, even as the distance to Grosvenor Square loomed in her mind. His hands clutched hers as she unfastened the first button of his falls.

"Rosalind, we cannot here. We risk being seen," he cautioned.

She placed a finger over his lips, silencing his protest. "I do not wish to hear again that we must refrain from what we desire. That we should not—that it is wrong." As she continued to unfasten his falls, his hands moved to her waist and held her close. "All I wish to hear from you, Your Grace, is three simple words: yes, we can."

He chuckled—a deep sound laden with wicked need—and she kissed him once more. Drawing her close, his tongue teased hers, his mouth devouring her as he removed her gown with deliberate care. His fingers slipped beneath, awakening her heated flesh, and she moaned, pressing into his embrace as desire overwhelmed her reason.

"You're so wet." he whispered, his voice breathless.

She nodded, moaning softly as he traced a

finger along her core. "I want you," she murmured.

Rosalind felt his arousal spring forth between them—erect and eager, mirroring her own desire. He gathered her in his arms, lifting her gently, and tried to lower her.

"Fuck, Rosalind," he murmured, his voice thick with passion.

She mewled, gripping his shoulders as she tried to take him in. He was large, firm—and perhaps even bigger than she had first assumed.

The carriage rocked to a halt, and she stumbled against him. The duke's eyes widened in alarm before he hastily gathered her and deposited her on the seat opposite, pulling his shirt down to cover himself just as the footman opened the door.

Rosalind rose unsteadily, her legs trembling, and paused at the door to allow Nathaniel time to regain his composure and right his attire. When his hand brushed gently against her back, she descended the steps and entered the house— more attuned to the heat of his presence than to his very form shadowing her steps.

Inside the mansion, they ascended the stairs together. Yet when it came time to part, Rosalind lingered before her door, hoping no servant would witness what she was determined to do.

"My suite of rooms is farther up the hall," the

duke announced, walking backward and distancing himself from her.

Rosalind grinned and followed, unwilling to let him escape yet again—never again. "I've never seen your room, Your Grace. Is it as grand as mine?" she inquired.

"Grander..." he replied, pausing at his door before swinging it wide. "Would you care to see it?"

Of course she did. She longed to behold it with desperate anticipation. Gliding past him, she ran her hand along his chest, eliciting a soft groan as he followed close behind, his lips brushing the nape of her neck.

In that charged moment—once the door closed—he came for her, claimed her, and made her his forever.

CHAPTER

TWENTY-NINE

Nathaniel attempted to rein in his desire, his need for Rosalind that was beyond control.

She sauntered past him, jasmine teasing his senses, before she turned and sat on the edge of the bed. He shut the door and leaned against it, snicking the lock to ensure no one interrupted them again.

His cock ached, and he threw off his coat and waistcoat, ripping his shirt over his head as he watched, transfixed, as Rosalind slipped her feet free of her slippers before sliding her gown up to her thighs and untying her silk stockings and removing them from her slim, long legs.

Christ, she would have him on his knees before the night was over, begging for mercy if he wasn't on guard.

She grinned, as if she knew what she was doing to him, and he shook his head, ripping his falls open and shoving his breeches down, kicking them off along with his boots without grace.

Her eyes widened as she took in his naked form, still standing against the door. He liked the heat that filled her eyes, and he reached for his cock, stroking it, working his manhood to stand to attention.

He glanced down—the head of his cock weeping—but it wasn't enough. He spat into the palm of his hand and worked it harder, felt his balls tighten as he grew close to coming.

"You're marvelous," she gasped, standing and reaching for the back of her gown, attempting to unclip her fastenings.

Nathaniel went to her, turned her about, and all but ripped the gown from her body. He freed her of her dress, her stays, and shift, leaving her in nothing but what he'd wanted from the very first moment.

Skin on skin, their bodies entwined, and each gave as much as they took.

He picked her up and laid her on the bed. She wiggled up to the pillows, her hair cascading over her shoulders. Hell, she had never looked more beautiful—and his. His from this day forward. His wife. His future duchess. He could barely wait for the morrow.

He kneeled between her legs and, watching her eyes, pressed her knees apart. She glistened under the candlelight in his room, and his mouth watered from the need to taste her.

"What are you doing, Nathaniel? Come to me," she said, reaching for him.

He shook his head, grinning. "All in good time, my love. Lie back and enjoy me. That's all I ask."

She did as he said and watched him, a light blush on her cheeks. He grinned, hoping her blush would be a lot darker by the time he'd finished with her.

He leaned down and licked along her cunny, teasing her flesh with his tongue as the first sweet taste of nectar that was Rosalind settled in his mouth. She gasped, her fingers threading through his hair before she clasped him to her, holding him against her weeping flesh. He fucked her with his mouth, teased her flesh, and sucked her nubbin until she was writhing against his face, finding her pleasure as much as he was giving her the same.

"Nathaniel, dear me," she moaned, arching her back as he slipped a finger into her heat, working her to a frenzy as his mouth suckled her to orgasm.

He felt the rush of her release, the convulsing of her flesh against his hand and mouth, and he did not stop until he had wrung every morsel of pleasure from her core.

She went lax beneath him, and he crawled to

kneel between her legs, slipping his cock against her cunny and rubbing her, teasing her with his manhood. Damn she felt good. So good.

"I'm going to fuck you now."

She nodded, excitement gleaming in her eyes. "I want you to." She pressed against him, seeking his cock. "You made me feel so good, Nathaniel."

"I'm going to make you feel better yet."

He guided his cock into her, watched her flesh part and stretch to take him fully. She moaned, reaching up to clasp the bedhead, pressing herself up to take him deeper. He groaned when he became fully sheathed. She was so tight and hot, fit him perfectly, and he braced himself, taking a calming breath to halt his need to come.

He wasn't a green lad, untested in bed. He knew what he was doing, and yet with Rosalind, he felt as though all of this was new—that his emotions, being what they were for her, made everything feel far more invigorating and real. Amazing.

He thrust into her, sinking to the hilt. He moaned, his body fighting for control. "You feel so good." He pumped into her, worked her flesh, and watched as indulgence flitted across her face. She wrapped her legs about his waist and pulled him deeper, rocking his world and tipping his control from its axis.

"I'm going to come if you continue to do

that," he managed to gasp, slowing his thrusts to prolong the pleasure.

She slipped a hand over one of her breasts and pinched her nipple. "Kiss me here," she begged him.

He groaned and slipped free, moving to suckle both her breasts, teasing her nipple with his tongue before twisting the other between his thumb and forefinger. She undulated beneath him, clearly enjoying his touch.

"Yes, Nathaniel. Ohh, that feels so good."

Hell yes it did. He reared back and flipped her onto her stomach, wrenching her hips up toward his cock. Her pert ass was showcased before him, and he teased her puckered hole with his cock before slipping it between her legs and pushing the head into her core.

"Don't tease me," she murmured against the pillows, turning her head to try to see what he was up to.

She was a sight to behold, and he knew what he was doing. He was stalling, attempting to prolong the pleasure, but it could not last forever—no matter how much he wanted it to. He wanted her too much to stretch out the night.

"I like to tease." He slipped himself into her, and she took him easily now, her wetness soothing his way.

He clasped her hips and pumped into her, deeper this way, and she moaned, calling out his name as he worked her to release. He reached around to tease her nubbin, rocking into her as he rolled his fingers against her flesh. She bucked against him, and he held her fast, not letting her get away, and kept her taking him, working him as they both roared toward release.

Her orgasm, when it came, took him by surprise with its severity. It wrung his cock, convulsed along his manhood, and milked him for everything he had.

"Rosalind," he roared, the weeks of pent-up need releasing in that one moment.

"Nathaniel," she moaned, gripping the bedding as if that were the only thing keeping her grounded.

He let her cunny drain him of every last ounce of his release, rolling his fingers against her flesh until she trembled in the wake of her orgasm.

He pulled out, and they slumped together onto the bed, side by side. He reached for her, pulling her into the crook of his arm, content and happy for the first time in months.

Her hand glided over his chest before settling around his cock, stroking his flaccid member.

"I think I shall like being married to you." She looked up to meet his eyes. "What else can you teach me? What else is there to do together?"

He groaned, knowing the time they would have together would never be long enough.

"There is lots to learn." He growled as her eyes lightened with curiosity.

"Will you teach me more tonight? I must know."

He nodded, knowing there was nothing he would deny her. The thought that she might take him into her mouth before the end of the evening made his cock twitch. "Any idea of what we may be able to do?" he asked, curious to know how much she might be privy to.

Her fingers wrapped about his member, and he gasped. "I'll leave that decision up to you," she said, leaning over to kiss his nipple. "But I'm a quick study, just so you know."

Nathaniel inwardly swore and thanked his luck at the same time. "Good, because there's much to study."

She grinned, moving to lie atop him. "Well then, we had better get learning. I want to know all."

He bet she did.

EPILOGUE

Twelve months later, London

Rosalind stood at the side of their Grosvenor Square ballroom floor, watching with pride—and not without a tear in her eye—as her sister, Lady Evangeline, commenced her coming-out dance with Nathaniel.

As the Duchess of Ravensmere and sponsor for her younger sibling, the months of preparation—and the enjoyment they both experienced leading up to her sister's debut—had been vastly different from her own, but she had suffered every tribulation to give her sister this wonderful day.

Evangeline was stunning this evening, and there was not a gentleman present who did not watch her with interest.

They would have to wait their turn, for now

Evangeline was busy, enjoying her first dance of the Season with someone who loved her as much as Rosalind did.

For several minutes, she watched, transfixed, until the set was over, and Nathaniel was relieved of his duty by Lord Wilkes for the next set.

Nathaniel strolled toward her, his cheeky grin making her stomach flutter and her pulse jump. The man had intoxicated her mind and soul, and she was his—utterly at his whim whenever he wished.

Not that she didn't also lord power over him. She'd learned many things in the last year, so much so that he was more in her power than the other way around.

"Thank you, my love," she said, as he took her hand and kissed the top of her gloved fingers.

He came to stand at her side and wrapped her arm through his. "She'll do well, I'm certain of it. She's beautiful and kind, just as you are, and I think she'll be well courted."

Rosalind looked up at Nathaniel, and he kissed her quickly, not caring who was around them. "Are you trying to get me into trouble again with the *ton*?" She laughed, not caring if they were ostracized altogether, knowing that would never occur.

After marrying the duke, whether Nathaniel was her guardian or not had not raised many brows—certainly not when there was a new duchess in society, a rich and powerful one whom society wanted to impress.

She had been welcomed back into their opulent world—not that Rosalind cared what they thought. Nor did Nathaniel, thankfully.

"Always, for then we can spend more time at home...alone," he said, wiggling his brows. "Oh, and before I forget to mention, my good friend from Eton has returned from Rome. He'll be joining us for supper this evening. He's been waylaid but will arrive to dine with us before enjoying the rest of the evening at the ball."

Rosalind raised her brow, having not heard of this friend before. "Whom do you speak of, my love? Have I met him before?" She turned back to Evangeline and watched to ensure she was safe and happy.

"No, but you know his mama—the dowager Countess St. George. Her son inherited the title some years ago. I think you'll like him. He's a good man."

"Oh, maybe he'll take a liking to Evangeline and court her?" she teased, having no idea if the gentleman was looking for a wife or not.

"Do not mention such a thing to your sister. I would not like to get her hopes up, but I am looking forward to you meeting him. He's quite the charmer."

"And good character I hope?"

"Of course." The duke nodded toward her

sibling. "Lord Felton seems to think he can dance with our girl. I'll have to have a word with him later this evening. Tell him to bugger the hell off."

Rosalind grinned, amused that Nathaniel held a grudge far longer than she did. As for grudges, he'd ensured she had not invited Lord Kelter or Lady Smithe this evening either.

"Let him be. Evangeline is not interested in him in any case. They were introduced some weeks ago in the park, remember, and she thought he looked like a toad."

"He does. She is not wrong." Nathaniel smirked, and then his eyes darkened with hunger. "You're beautiful this evening. Have I told you that yet?"

She felt a blush kiss her cheeks and nudged him with her shoulder. "You have. But I'm always willing to hear your compliments again. I so adore them."

"Mmmm, as I adore you." He looked about before leaning close to ensure privacy. "Should we excuse ourselves for an hour or so? I think the ball will run smoothly without us, do you not think?"

Rosalind laughed and slapped his chest with her fan. "I do not think so, no, Your Grace. Now, off you go and be a good brother-in-law and host. Ensure the men are on their best behavior toward my sister. We Ravensmeres have a standard to uphold."

He winked and bussed her cheek before moving away. "I'm at your service, Your Grace."

She grinned, drinking in the sight of him as he strolled back into the throng of guests. "As I am at yours, Duke."

DON'T MISS TAMARA'S OTHER ROMANCE SERIES

Heiress

Diamond of the Season

Treasure of the Ton

Jewel of the Ball

1777 Society

One Night in London

Midnight in Mayfair

An Evening to Remember

Dalliance and Dukes

My Virtuous Duke

My Notorious Rogue

My Ruthless Beau

The Wayward Yorks

A Wager with a Duke

My Reformed Rogue

Wild, Wild, Duke

In the Duke of Time

Duke Around and Find Out

The Wayward Woodvilles

A Duke of a Time

On a Wild Duke Chase

Speak of the Duke

Every Duke has a Silver Lining

One Day my Duke Will Come

Surrender to the Duke

My Reckless Earl

Brazen Rogue

The Notorious Lord Sin

Wicked in My Bed

League of Unweddable Gentlemen

Tempt Me, Your Grace

Hellion at Heart

Dare to be Scandalous

To Be Wicked With You

Kiss Me, Duke

The Marquess is Mine

Kiss the Wallflower

A Midsummer Kiss

A Kiss at Mistletoe

A Kiss in Spring

To Fall For a Kiss

A Duke's Wild Kiss

To Kiss a Highland Rose

To Marry a Rogue

Only an Earl Will Do

Only a Duke Will Do

Only a Viscount Will Do

Only a Marquess Will Do

Only a Lady Will Do

Lords of London

To Bedevil a Duke

To Madden a Marquess

To Tempt an Earl

To Vex a Viscount

To Dare a Duchess

To Marry a Marchioness

Royal House of Atharia

To Dream of You

A Royal Proposition

Forever My Princess

A Time Traveler's Highland Love

To Conquer a Scot

To Save a Savage Scot

To Win a Highland Scot

A Stolen Season

A Stolen Season

A Stolen Season: Bath

A Stolen Season: London

Scandalous London

A Gentleman's Promise

A Captain's Order

A Marriage Made in Mayfair

High Seas & High Stakes

His Lady Smuggler

Her Gentleman Pirate

A Wallflower's Christmas Wreath

Daughters Of The Gods

Banished

Guardian

Fallen

Stand Alone Books

Defiant Surrender

A Brazen Agreement

To Sin with Scandal

Outlaws

ABOUT THE AUTHOR

Tamara is an Australian author who grew up in an old mining town in country South Australia, where her love of history was founded. So much so, she made her darling husband travel to the UK for their honeymoon, where she dragged him from one historical monument and castle to another.

A mother of three, her two little gentlemen in the making, a future lady (she hopes) keep her busy in the real world, but whenever she gets a moment's peace she loves to write romance novels in an array of genres, including regency, medieval and time travel.

Made in United States
North Haven, CT
01 August 2025